CHITA

CHITA

A Memory of Last Island

Lafcadio Hearn

Introduction by Jefferson Humphries
Edited by Delia LaBarre

University Press of Mississippi / *Jackson*

www.upress.state.ms.us

Designed by Todd Lape

The University Press of Mississippi is a member
of the Association of American University Presses.

First published in 1888 in *Harper's New Monthly Magazine*.
First book edition published in 1889 by Harper's Brothers.
Preface and Introduction copyright © 2003 by University
Press of Mississippi
Manufactured in the United States
of America

11 10 09 08 07 06 05 04 03 4 3 2 1
∞
Library of Congress Cataloging-in-Publication Data

Hearn, Lafcadio, 1850–1904.
Chita : a memory of Last Island / Lafcadio Hearn ; introduction by Jefferson Humphries ; edited by Delia LaBarre.
p. cm.
ISBN 1-57806-558-5 (alk. paper)
1. Fathers and daughters—Fiction. 2. Missing children—
Fiction. 3. Yellow fever—Fiction. 4. Hurricanes—Fiction.
5. Physicians—Fiction. 6. Louisiana—Fiction. 7. Islands—
Fiction. I. LaBarre, Delia. II. Title.
PS1917 .C513 2003
813'.4—dc21   2002013632

British Library Cataloging-in-Publication Data available

CONTENTS

PREFACE

This new edition of *Chita: A Memory of Last Island* is issued at a time when we in Louisiana, and other states that border the Gulf of Mexico, are increasingly aware of the disappearance of our barrier islands and coastal marshlands—gradual and sudden losses that increasingly endanger economies and cultures of the Deepest South, even threatening the very lives of its inhabitants. Descriptions of these losses we face today but that were written in the late 1880s by Lafcadio Hearn, during his months on Grande Isle, may be surprising to readers unfamiliar with Hearn's works. But those familiar with them are no more surprised by the relevance of *Chita* to Louisiana's present-day realities than by his other writings from his New Orleans period, 1877 to 1888, that seem all at once quaint and timeless. This is not without also acknowledging that old French adage that has always been descriptive of

Louisiana: The more things change the more they stay
the same.

Unfortunately this is not the case with our coasts:

> Forever the yellow Mississippi strives to build; forever
> the sea struggles to destroy;—and amid their eternal strife
> the islands and the promontories change shape, more
> slowly, but not less fantastically, than the clouds of heaven.

No matter how many times we read *Chita*, Hearn
still has the power to startle us with the beauty of his
expressions we find here, even when they describe the
erosion of land and culture. However, just as startling
are his insights of regeneration, represented by the
blending of languages and cultures in South
Louisiana—the "creolization" that Hearn experienced
himself during his Louisiana decade.

But what exactly is a Creole? This question has
caused good-humored responses and contentious ran-
cor. Hearn's answer has been according to the former
attitude, and despite efforts (including some quite
recent) to discredit (mainly by ignoring) what Hearn
wrote on the subject in New Orleans in early 1878, "*Los
Criollos*," Hearn's explanation is still the most reliable
place to begin.

What is repeatedly missed by many writers and
scholars bent on dictating which individuals and groups
creole can be applied to and how historians should use it
today in discussions of the past is that the term was
always a *relative* one. For the Creoles of Louisiana it
denoted an individual or group by distinguishing it

from others, others which varied over time. As outside forces encroached upon the Creole world, more and more people and products within it were labeled *créole*—French from the Spanish infinitive *criar*, meaning to raise or to rear—to deliniate them from others: foreign French or Spanish, and later American; free people of color without European ancestry; slaves who did not speak French or the patois; foods and livestock, architecture, and an entire way of life. Thus, through a unitary nomenclature the boundaries of the larger Creole cultural territory were fortified as a defensive extension of the expression *Vive la difference!*

When Hearn arrived in New Orleans he found descendants of various groups from the colonial and antebellum eras who called themselves Creoles. He not only recognized them all as such, he studied and explained the Creole cultural phenomena to the larger world. Perhaps in the near future more scholars will engage in serious studies of the historical evidence regarding Creoles of the Western Hemisphere, and we will come to a better understanding of those of Louisiana. But Hearn's articles on Louisiana Creoles, including "*Los Criollos,*" collected in S. Frederick Starr's *Inventing New Orleans: Writings of Lafcadio Hearn*, also published by University Press of Mississippi (2001), remain the most relevant explanations of what it means to be *Creole*, a term that occurs no less than fifteen times in the text of *Chita*, with almost as many definitions.

From the pages of *Chita* the reader will absorb Hearn's further views on the meaning of this mysterious word that shifts and changes shape in language according to internal and external forces that affected the people of a remote edge of the world. *Chita* is the culmination of all Hearn's studies and writings while in Louisiana and is indeed the quintessential Creole novel, even in its demi-novel form, like the Crescent City shaping itself around a curve of the Mississippi, or a tiny barrier island that bears the brunt of the sea's wrath, with a stunning tale to relate—if it survives.

Chita was first published in 1888 in *Harper's New Monthly Magazine*. Hearn made a number of minor changes for the first book edition published by Harper's Brothers the following year. The latter is the source of the text for this edition. Several footnotes have been added to assist readers unfamiliar with South Louisiana or the foreign languages that appear in the text without translation.

Hearn's dedication, "to Dr. Rudolfo Matas," included in the first few Harper's Brothers editions, has been retained. The New Orleans surgeon Dr. Matas was Lafcadio Hearn's friend and confidante, his personal physician, and the consultant on the Spanish language in *Chita* and the yellow fever symptoms Hearn describes in the story. Hearn was not alone in his reverence for Matas, who outlived him by more than fifty years: In its centennial commemorative edition of 6 June 1977, marking its beginning from that of the *Daily City Item*, the New Orleans *States-Item* named Dr. Rudolph Matas as the "Man of the *States-Item* Century," leading twelve other "Giants in an era of challenge for N.O." Dr. Matas "was the most effective single person in the historic campaign that wiped out the dread scourge of yellow fever in New Orleans." In 1901, after Walter Reed and his associates proved the mosquito was responsible for the spread of the "Invisible Destruction," as Hearn calls the disease in *Chita*, Dr. Matas led the Orleans Parish Medical Society in establishing a committee to assess the mosquito population in the city, which led to an aggressive mosquito abatement program and ultimately the end to outbreaks of the disease whose toll, besides the immeasurable emotional, amounted to 175 thousand lives lost between 1796 and 1905 and an economy, also devastated during the nineteenth century by the Civil War and twelve years of Reconstruction government, further crippled by quarantines. Hearn witnessed the yellow fever epidemic of 1878, the third worst, during the first summer after his arrival in New Orleans. The suffering it caused made an indelible impression on him. If there was anything Hearn respected more than literary or scientific genius, it was people who survived great suffering and who did so with dignity. He found many such people in subtropical, post-Reconstruction New Orleans in the latter part of the nineteenth century.

This first edition of *Chita* in the twenty-first century was sparked by S. Frederick Starr while gathering the texts for *Inventing New Orleans*. Few non-Louisiana natives since Lafcadio Hearn have contributed as much to the cultural understanding and appreciation of New Orleans as Dr. Starr has. It is with pleasure and a sense of privilege that we continue his Lafcadio Hearn initiative by bringing this literary gem, a universal tale in a South Louisiana setting, to readers everywhere, but especially to those in Louisiana; in Mississippi and Alabama, who share Louisiana Creole history; and in Louisiana's other Gulf Coast neighbors with fragile coasts and vulnerable barrier islands, Texas and Florida.

We are grateful to Grant J. Dupré, and Dupré's Printing of Baton Rouge for contributions to the tasks and technological overhead involved in preparing the text for this edition. The staff of LSU's Hill Memorial Library, were, as always, helpful in the research for this volume, as were the staff of the Williams Research Center of the Historic New Orleans Collection, especially Pamela Arceneaux and gift shop manager Diane Plauché. The Louisiana Collection of the Louisiana State Library and its staff provided valuable sources, and the facilities of that library and Bluebonnet Branch of the East Baton Rouge Parish Public Library provided vital services.

Also due a note of gratitude is historian Robert Becker, Louisiana State University, and Marc Levitan, director of the LSU Hurricane Center, for their support of the *Chita* project; John Mastrigianakos, assistant professor of Italian in LSU's foreign languages department; Ivor van Heerden, assistant director of the LSU Hurricane Center, formerly of the Center for Coastal, Energy, and Environmental Resources of LSU and author of its proposal *A Long-term, Comprehensive Management Plan for Coastal Louisiana to Ensure Sustainable Biological Productivity, Economic Growth, and the Continued Existence of its Unique Culture and Heritage*. We are also appreciative of assistance from Amber Middleton and the Friends of the Cabildo in New Orleans; Robert Gilmore Robinson; Ann Russo, visual arts director of the Division of Arts, Louisiana Department of Culture, Recreation and Tourism; and Jennifer Webb.

This reissue of *Chita* has been encouraged by a number of others closely involved in the works of Lafcadio Hearn as professors, writers, and librarians: Maurice duQuesnay, professor of English and Louisiana literature and director of the Flora Levy Series in the Humanities, University of Louisiana at Lafayette; Bill Manery, director of Special Collections, Howard-Tilton Memorial Library at Tulane University, which houses the Lafcadio Hearn Collection; folklorist Frank de Caro, LSU professor emeritus; and Ben Forkner, professor of American and Irish literature, University of Angers in France.

We have had the good fortune of finding Jeff Humphries in New Orleans, on sabbatical from his chairmanship of LSU's Center for French Studies and willing to devote himself to the introduction to this edition of *Chita*. His professor was the esteemed critic of southern literature Arlin Turner, who wrote the introduction to the 1969 critical edition of *Chita*. From Dr. Humphries' vantage point of his balcony in the Vieux Carré of New Orleans, as a French literature and a Japan scholar, as well as a poet, he gives us new vistas of *Chita*, which contribute to a better understanding of this novella and its place in world literature. It is hoped that this volume serves as a further invitation to others—the general reading public and scholars from various disciplines—to "rediscover" Hearn's Louisiana works, much as Japan scholars are reassessing Hearn's Japanese writings, as described in *Rediscovering Lafcadio Hearn: Japanese Legends, Life, and Cultures* (edited by Sukehiro Hirakawa, Kent, UK: Global Oriental, 1997).

Whether readers are discovering Lafcadio Hearn for the first time in these pages or rediscovering him, we are fortunate to have the blessings and support of the Historic New Orleans Collection and publications director Lou Hoffman in presenting this edition and recognizing *Chita* as a Louisiana, national, and international literary treasure to be cherished and preserved for present and future readers.

We are deeply indebted to Seetha Srinivasan, director of University Press of Mississippi, for taking a special interest in the Louisiana works of Lafcadio Hearn and publishing the Press's second volume of Hearn's writings in this, the twenty-first century, as we read toward the centennial of the death of Lafcadio Hearn: 19 September 2004.

Perhaps by the Lafcadio Hearn Centennial the fate of the house on the corner of Cleveland and S. Robertson Streets in New Orleans will be resolved favorably toward its preservation as an especially significant historic site. It was here Lafcadio Hearn lived during his last years in the city; it was here that he finished *Chita*, following his return from Grande Isle. At this time the structure languishes precariously at a legal corner; its fate is uncertain. As one might expect, in Louisiana protection of barrier islands, restoration of coastal marshlands, and preservation of historic landmarks— even important jazz sites such as the Halfway House in

New Orleans, that music's natal city—are often met with great resistance. The city of New Orleans belatedly bemoans the destruction of the birthplace and home of Louis Armstrong. It has only been in the past year that this native genius has received (posthumously) long due recognition by the city.

Dr. Bill Manery, Director of Special Collections at Tulane University in New Orleans, names the three most significant cultural figures of New Orleans as French Creole composer Louis Moreau Gottschalk, jazz trumpeter Louis Armstrong, and journalist and writer Lafcadio Hearn. The majority of Louisianians have heard of neither Gottschalk nor Hearn. Our Japanese friends have been particularly miffed by the continued negligence of Lafcadio Hearn, whose association with Matsue, New Orleans' sister city in Japan, has made it a major tourist attraction.

In early August 2001, during the first Louis Armstrong Conference and Festival, a small group of Japanese made a pilgrimage to New Orleans to find Lafcadio Hearn's Louisiana. They traveled to Grande Isle, where Hearn wrote *Chita*. Back in New Orleans, they went to the corner of Cleveland and S. Robertson. By this time the two-storied brick house was vacant and boarded up, so they were unable to step up the winding stairway Hearn had climbed to reach his balconied room, where he had labored over the final manuscript of *Chita* before leaving the city for the West Indies and, two years later, Japan.

The leader of the group of pilgrims was Kenji Zenimoto, professor of international studies at Shimane University in Matsue, president of Japan's Lafcadio

Hearn Society, vice-president of the Japan-Ireland Society. Had he lived longer he undoubtedly would have striven with us, in the same spirit of international cooperation and exchange that pervaded his life's work, to preserve this house as a Lafcadio Hearn museum.

We dedicate this edition to that spirit and to the memory of Professor Kenji Zenimoto.

—Delia LaBarre
Baton Rouge, May 2002

INTRODUCTION

*Travelling south from New Orleans
to the Islands you pass through
a strange land into a strange sea
by various winding waterways.*

The two most important words in this delightful little narrative may be among the first: "last"—as in "Last
Island"—and "strange." "Last" is perilously close to
"lost," and the story is one of disastrous loss as well as
of closure. In 1856 the Gulf of Mexico reared up and
devoured L'Île dernière, pretty much whole, with most
of its inhabitants and wealthy vacationers. There were
a few survivors, those who made it to the relative safety
of Captain Abraham Smith's boat, tied up at anchor in
a protected inlet—even a cow and perhaps a few other
domestic animals outlasted the storm, according to the
New Orleans papers. But nearly all who saw the water
rise up through the floor of the island's grand hotel did

not live to see that water recede. A few seconds after the sea reached up through the floorboards, the structure—along with every other one on the island—collapsed, taking at least two hundred people with it.

It is a horrific but mesmerizing story, an image that compels our attention as it terrifies. Not unlike the story of the *Titanic*, the "greatest, fastest, most unsinkable ship ever built" whose human-wrought elegance seems all the more beautiful and romantic because we know it was doomed, or the *Edmund Fitzgerald*, the great cargo vessel that was swallowed by Lake Superior in the 1970s. But there is a difference: those two ships were made by men to withstand Nature's onslaughts; l'Île dernière was itself a natural phenomenon, very much defined by the vagaries of time and the elements. We might call Last Island a meteorological disaster. Certainly the sea was rough for days before the storm hit the island, and the signs were clear enough that the old sea captain, Smith, took precautions. Perhaps—probably, even—most of the lives lost could have been spared by the modern science of weather-forecasting. But this does not alter the events of 1856.

Visiting Grand Isle many years later, Lafcadio Hearn saw in it what many have seen since, and now—it seems similarly doomed, and all the more charming for being so. New Orleans itself, with its improbably high levees holding back the great hoary river whose hoary brown waters sometimes rise up higher than the roof of the French Market in the old French Quarter, derives more than a little of its allure from a similar aura of precariousness, of beauty *and* sadness, as Hearn said,

beauty in sadness. Somehow, the vicissitudes of temporal existence seem more palpable here, as well as more
poetical, more charming. It was the proto-southern
writer, Edgar Allan Poe, who had declared in his "Phi-
losophy of Composition" that there was nothing in the
world more poetical than the death of a beautiful
woman. Hearn saw in New Orleans the very poetical
loveliness of a beautiful, tropical bride, laid out in her
casket after an untimely death. But New Orleans and,
up to now, Grand Isle are among the living dead, making them the perfect backdrop for Anne Rice's post-
modern gothic novels and Poppy Z. Brite's more lurid
celebrations of the macabre, not to mention the private
fantasies of countless Goth kids who pass nightly
beneath my balcony on lower Decatur Street. No
where else is Allan Tate's ironical invitation in "Ode to
the Confederate Dead" so emphatically accepted:
"Shall we set up the grave in the house, The ravenous
grave?" In New Orleans, of course, the graves are
houses, and the city itself is perhaps a *Titanic* waiting
to happen (the meteorologists tell us so); those final
moments may however be prolonged indefinitely by
human ingenuity (the Corps of Engineers)—God
knows I hope so. But the fact remains that this aspect
of the city, what I have called its precariousness, is as
indispensable to its beauty as its courtyards and iron
gates.

It was Marcel Proust who said that "the only true
paradises are the ones that have been lost," a sentiment
that the ruin-loving John Ruskin—translated by Proust
into French and much-admired by Hearn—would

have loved. In his necrophiliac obsession with cultures on the verge of disappearance, his fascination with the metaphysics of time and space, the conundrum of cultural and temporal entropy, Hearn embraced the same baroque aesthetic as Proust and Ruskin, two writers to whom he is not compared often enough. Hearn was not convinced that things did not get worse instead of better over time. He was fascinated by theories that man had not only existed in the Tertiary period but had a greater cranial capacity in that earlier incarnation. Beauty for Hearn, whether the remnants of "Tertiary Epoch" femininity surviving in a young Basque inhabitant of Grand Isle, the dilapidated grandeur of the old Creole houses with their dormer windows and facades right on the street, or the "old Japan" under assault from within, by Japanese bent on modernization. Hearn found beauty and civilization in the past, not the future. The future would be governed by comfort, convenience, and democracy, and these were not, in Hearn's view, likely to produce anything very pretty. (He described himself as a demophobe.) There is a certain irony here, because Hearn preferred the company of ordinary people to society folk; it was the latter—who were far less numerous—whom he blamed for the tasteless encroachments of modernity.

Hearn was steeped in the aesthetic principles of nineteenth-century French "decadence," exemplified by poets such as Baudelaire and Mallarmé, who saw the bourgeois modernity growing up around them as crass, and beauty as something necessarily odd, strange, weird, exotic within its modern context. Beauty in such a world is increasingly exceptional, and the love of beauty is more and more inseparable from a love of the exotic. Since the great ages of beauty are in the past, exoticism itself becomes a form of nostalgia. The love of New Orleans and of the Franco-Spanish Creole world that emanated out from it, in plantations along the River Road and "strange, last/lost" settlements along the coast, defines Hearn's Louisiana. New Orleans is of course still the capital of what we might call exotic, even "strange" Louisiana, the Louisiana embraced by Hearn. The rest of the South in the twentieth century bears comparison to Japan in the nineteenth, with its shame of its own unique eccentricities and its great haste to embrace the new: Baton Rouge, for instance, has been transformed by Protestant immigrants from Mississippi and northern Louisiana from a funky, quiet backwater into the sprawling, shiny, suburban utopia of the French decadents' worst nightmares, a place where beauty is defined in terms of comfort, convenience, safety, and affluence. (A parodic version of this reality can be seen in the sets of evangelical Christian television programs: everything brand new, bright, and synthetic.) These two cities—New Orleans and Baton Rouge—are in many respects the yin and yang not only of Louisiana, or even of the South, but of America itself. New Orleans today is loved by people from all over the United States and the world who love it for the very same anomalous things that Hearn loved it for—its antiquated, even dilapidated beauty, its sultry, stubborn inefficiency, its precariousness. It is hated by many of its own natives for the same qualities ("Nothing works; no one cares"). L'Île dernière is a metaphor, in Hearn's imagination, for New Orleans itself in all its sad, fatal beauty, and Chita is an allegory of that beauty's persistence, even in the midst of inclement forces—as well as of Hearn's own odd odyssey.

Indeed the resonances with Hearn's own life story are striking, and generally ignored by critics. He is said to have heard the tale—a "true" story—over dinner at the residence of George Washington Cable, one of Hearn's first and best literary friends in New Orleans. According to the story, "Chita" belonged to a distinguished Creole family, and was the only one of her immediate relatives to survive the storm at Last Island. She was taken in by a community of simple fishermen, only to be recognized by a white Creole years later and brought to New Orleans to receive a proper young Creole lady's upbringing in the convent. Not finding the nuns or the elegant Franco-Spanish society of the city to her taste, she fled back whence she had come, married a fisherman, and "lives somewhere down there now,—the mother of multitudinous children," as Hearn wrote in a letter to a friend in Philadelphia. He changed the story told to him in one important respect, omitting Chita's recognition and "rescue" by her true relations. Why?

Hearn himself was, in a sense, the product of a "natural" conflagration. His father, Charles, was a surgeon in the British military and his mother, Rosa Cassimati, a beautiful young woman from the Greek island of Cytherea, where the goddess of love herself, Aphrodite, is said to have emerged from the sea, and where Paris and Helen of Troy hid from the latter's husband. Charles Hearn fell passionately in love with Rosa's exotic looks and fiery spirit, and they became lovers long before they were married, having two children out of wedlock—extremely scandalous behavior in Rosa's tradition-bound noble island family and to the Anglo-Protestant Hearns of Dublin. They were eventually married anyway. But Charles Hearn's passion for the young woman did not survive for long his return to Ireland from a stint in the British West Indies. Rosa was subject to spells of extreme depression and to frequent outbursts of uncontrollable temper. The very tempestuousness that had fascinated him at first now chipped away at Charles's affection for Rosa. Returning in poor health from the Crimean War, he had the marriage annulled on a legal technicality. Rosa was remarried in the Greek islands, but the two surviving children (a third child, James, had been born while Charles was away in the Crimea) were sent to live in Ireland with Charles Hearn's eccentric, wealthy aunt, Sarah Brenane. The "storm" for Lafcadio consisted of this exile from the warm exotic islands of his birth and from his mother, the memory of whom he always idealized—though there is evidence that she had abused him during her fits of depression. Lafcadio had been born into a well-to-do Victorian family (the Hearns), but he was never happy with them. Sarah Brenane's harsh northern European Catholicism (she was the most zealous of converts) was a stark contrast to the simple, almost pagan faith of Rosa Cassimati's Greek

Orthodoxy. As soon as he was able, Lafcadio left behind his father's family, with its stale proprieties and cold hypocrisies, for the new and bustling United States. It might be said that the storm of his parents' union—as inexorably doomed to dissolution as Last Island in 1856—had cast Lafcadio on a sea of exile, only to find himself more at home than ever among the rough informalities and polyculturalism of the Americas. So why would he have left out Chita's rediscovery and reintroduction to white Creole society? Perhaps because it had no correlate in his own story. The Hearns had never truly accepted or sought to assimilate Lafcadio. He had never been for them anything much more than the weird fruit of Charles Hearn's youthful indiscretion.

What Chita loved in the simple life of the Gulf Island fisherman who adopted her is very close to what Hearn loved about Louisiana: its lush, but simple, anachronistic eccentricities. It was the odd, the weird, and the lurid that he loved wherever he went, but the flavor of these in Louisiana—unlike that of the tallow district of Cincinnati—was leavened with warm breezes and the scent of gardenias.

Like Flaubert's *Madame Bovary, Chita* was inspired by a factual story. Does this make it a work of journalism, the production of a great "feature" newspaperman? I sympathize with my journalist friends who wish to claim Hearn as one of their own, but I fear the case cannot be plausibly sustained. It would not be more inaccurate to say that the poet Wallace Stevens was an insurance man (he was an executive with a large Hart-

ford insurance firm), or that Marcel Proust was a journalist because he published in *Le Figaro*. Hearn was
nothing if not a literary man and a "high" literary one
at that. Then as now, there are virtually no enterprises
that will pay for literary production, and Hearn
worked for newspapers to keep body and soul together.
The kind of writing he did for them would not find a
place in any twentieth-century newspaper. He
described it himself in the New Orleans *Item* of 28
March 1881 as "brief stories whose effect depends
wholly upon uniqueness of conception—sketches
which although suggested by fact are moulded and colored by imagination alone." It makes more sense to say
that Hearn offers a noble example to all those newspaper feature writers who have literary aspirations than to
say that Hearn himself was a journalist.

Like Flaubert, like the French poet Theophile Gautier whose work he translated, Hearn was a wordsmith.
In Gautier he admired "perfection of melody . . .
warmth of word-colouring . . . a voluptuous delicacy
which no English poet has ever approached." The right
word (*le mot juste*) was of utmost importance to him,
and the precise musical quality of a phrase, its rhythm,
flow, and cadence. He wished, above all else, to create
what he called "a poetical prose." One of his friends
wrote that during his work on *Chita* he would "come
in in his peculiar timid way a dozen times in a
forenoon, to ask the effect of a change of a single
word." Like Flaubert, who was famous for writing page
upon page in order to arrive at a single satisfactory sen-
tence, Hearn sought to achieve "the visible mainte-

nance of a purpose in the choice of words." But unlike Flaubert, who strove for an apparent simplicity of style, Hearn's taste was decidedly baroque. "I shall try," he wrote, "to be at once voluptuous and elegant, like a colonnade in a mosque of Cordova."

His influences in literature were all French, and another principal one was Pierre Loti, who had traveled to many exotic places during his naval service and in whose works the scene itself becomes a protagonist. Loti's exoticism was reflected in an ornate style that took precedence over plot and character. Much the same is true of Hearn's writing, in *Chita* and elsewhere. Hearn was not naive about his penchant for the exotic, yet he did not apologize for it either. "There is such a delightful pleasantness about the *first* relations with people in strange places," he wrote, "but after a while the illusion is over." It was not the reality that mattered to him but the illusion itself, because it was in the illusion that beauty resided, and he followed the French symbolist poets in believing that beauty was all. It is too easy, and just plain wrong, to dismiss Hearn as a "colonialist" writer, a literary voice of "imperialism" because he embraced his impressions, even though these could not withstand the pressures of prolonged familiarity. This misses the point. In his writing and his language he created something extraordinary where perhaps there was only a very ordinary thing, and by allowing others to see what he thought he was seeing, he *invented*—or resurrected?—a New Orleans, a Creole Louisiana, an Old Japan, that were on the verge of disappearing forever. It might be said then that he empowered cultures in danger of succumbing to the pressures of colonialism and "progress" to endure in their old ways. For, in fact, we cannot see a thing in reality until we can see it in our minds, and this is what Hearn's writing allows us to do. The birds of Audubon's paintings are far more strange and poetical than they appear in nature, and yet now the real birds are infused with a poetry that comes from Audubon's vision of them. As Robert Penn Warren put it, "He [Audubon] put them where they are, and that is where we see them: in our imagination." The same can be said of what Hearn did for Louisiana and for Japan. Neither would be as they are today without his vision of them and his literary expression of that vision.

CHITA

Je suis la vaste mêlée,—
Reptile, étant l'onde; ailée,
Étant le vent,—
Force et fuite, haine et vie,
Houle immense, poursuivie
Et poursuivant.[1]

—Victor Hugo

---

1. I am the vast fray—
Reptilian, for I am a wave; winged,
    for I am wind,—
Force and flight, hatred and life,
Immense swell, pursued
    and pursuing. [<u>trans</u>. Jefferson
Humphries]

Part I

THE LEGEND OF
L'ÎLE DERNIÈRE

I.

Travelling south from New Orleans to the Islands, you pass through a strange land into a strange sea, by various winding waterways. You can journey to the Gulf by lugger if you please; but the trip may be made much more rapidly and agreeably on some one of those light, narrow steamers, built especially for bayou-travel, which usually receive passengers at a point not far from the foot of old Saint-Louis Street, hard by the sugar-landing, where there is ever a pushing and flocking of steam-craft—all striving for place to rest their white breasts against the levée, side by side,—like great weary swans. But the miniature steam-boat on which you engage passage to the Gulf never lingers long in the

Mississippi: she crosses the river, slips into some canal-mouth, labors along the artificial channel awhile, and then leaves it with a scream of joy, to puff her free way down many a league of heavily shadowed bayou. Perhaps thereafter she may bear you through the immense silence of drenched rice-fields, where the yellow-green level is broken at long intervals by the black silhouette of some irrigating machine;—but, whichever of the five different routes be pursued, you will find yourself more than once floating through sombre mazes of swamp-forest,—past assemblages of cypresses all hoary with the parasitic *tillandsia*,[2] and grotesque as gatherings of fetich-gods. Ever from river or from lakelet the steamer glides again into canal or bayou,—from bayou or canal once more into lake or bay; and sometimes the swamp-forest visibly thins away from these shores into wastes of reedy morass where, even of breathless nights, the quaggy soil trembles to a sound like thunder of breakers on a coast: the storm-roar of billions of reptile voices chanting in cadence,—rhythmically surging in stupendous *crescendo* and *diminuendo*,—a monstrous and appalling chorus of frogs! . . .

Panting, screaming, scraping her bottom over the sand-bars,—all day the little steamer strives to reach the grand blaze of blue open water below the marsh-lands; and perhaps she may be fortunate enough to enter the Gulf about the time of sunset. For the sake of passengers, she travels by day only; but there are other vessels which make the journey also by night—threading the

2. genus to which Spanish moss—actually an air plant and not parasitic—belongs

bayou-labyrinths winter and summer: sometimes steering by the North Star,—sometimes feeling the way with poles in the white season of fogs,—sometimes, again, steering by that Star of Evening which in our sky glows like another moon, and drops over the silent lakes as she passes a quivering trail of silver fire.

Shadows lengthen; and at last the woods dwindle away behind you into thin bluish lines;—land and water alike take more luminous color;—bayous open into broad passes;—lakes link themselves with sea-bays;—and the ocean-wind bursts upon you,—keen, cool, and full of light. For the first time the vessel begins to swing,—rocking to the great living pulse of the tides. And gazing from the deck around you, with no forest walls to break the view, it will seem to you that the low land must have once been rent asunder by the sea, and strewn about the Gulf in fantastic tatters. . . .

Sometimes above a waste of wind-blown prairie-cane you see an oasis emerging,—a ridge or hillock heavily umbraged with the rounded foliage of ever-green oaks:—a *chênière*. And from the shining flood also kindred green knolls arise,—pretty islets, each with its beach-girdle of dazzling sand and shells, yellow-white,—and all radiant with semi-tropical foliage, myrtle and palmetto, orange and magnolia. Under their emerald shadows curious little villages of pal-metto huts are drowsing, where dwell a swarthy population of Orientals,—Malay fishermen, who speak the Spanish-Creole of the Philippines as well as their own Tagal, and perpetuate in Louisiana the Catholic traditions of the Indies. There are girls in those unfamiliar villages worthy to inspire any statuary,—beautiful with the beauty of ruddy bronze,—gracile as the palmettoes that sway above them. . . . Farther seaward you may also pass a Chinese settlement: some queer camp of wooden dwellings clustering around a vast platform that stands above the water upon a thousand piles;— over the miniature wharf you can scarcely fail to observe a white sign-board painted with crimson ideographs. The great platform is used for drying fish in the sun; and the fantastic characters of the sign, literally translated, mean: "*Heap—Shrimp—Plenty.*" . . . And finally all the land melts down into desolations of sea-marsh, whose stillness is seldom broken, except by the melancholy cry of long-legged birds, and in wild seasons by that sound which shakes all shores when the weird Musician of the Sea touches the bass keys of his mighty organ. . . .

II.

Beyond the sea-marshes a curious archipelago lies. If you travel by steamer to the sea-islands to-day, you are tolerably certain to enter the Gulf by Grande Pass— skirting Grande Terre, the most familiar island of all, not so much because of its proximity as because of its great crumbling fort and its graceful pharos: the stationary White-Light of Barataria. Otherwise the place is bleakly uninteresting: a wilderness of wind-swept grasses and sinewy weeds waving away from a thin beach ever speckled with drift and decaying things,—

worm-riddled timbers, dead porpoises. Eastward the russet level is broken by the columnar silhouette of the light-house, and again, beyond it, by some puny scrub-timber, above which rises the angular ruddy mass of the old brick fort, whose ditches swarm with crabs, and whose sluiceways are half choked by obsolete cannon-shot, now thickly covered with incrustation of oyster shells. . . . Around all the gray circling of a shark-haunted sea. . . .

Sometimes of autumn evenings there, when the hollow of heaven flames like the interior of a chalice, and waves and clouds are flying in one wild rout of broken gold,—you may see the tawny grasses all covered with something like husks,—wheat-colored husks,—large, flat, and disposed evenly along the lee-side of each swaying stalk, so as to present only their edges to the wind. But, if you approach, those pale husks all break open to display strange splendors of scarlet and seal-brown, with arabesque mottlings in white and black: they change into wondrous living blossoms, which detach themselves before your eyes and rise in air, and flutter away by thousands to settle down farther off, and turn into wheat-colored husks once more . . . a whirling flower-drift of sleepy butterflies!

Southwest, across the pass, gleams beautiful Grande Isle: primitively a wilderness of palmetto (*latanier*);—then drained, diked, and cultivated by Spanish sugar-planters; and now familiar chiefly as a bathing-resort. Since the war the ocean reclaimed its own;—the cane-fields have degenerated into sandy plains, over which tramways wind to the smooth beach;—the plantation-

residences have been converted into rustic hotels, and
the negro-quarters remodelled into villages of cozy cottages for the reception of guests. But with its imposing
groves of oak, its golden wealth of orange-trees, its
odorous lanes of oleander, its broad grazing-meadows
yellow-starred with wild camomile, Grande Isle
remains the prettiest island of the Gulf; and its loveliness is exceptional. For the bleakness of Grande Terre is
reiterated by most of the other islands,—Caillou, Cas-
setête, Calumet, Wine Island, the twin Timbaliers,
Gull Island, and the many islets haunted by the gray
pelican,—all of which are little more than sand-bars
covered with wiry grasses, prairie-cane, and scrub-timber. Last Island (*L'Île Dernière*),—well worthy a long
visit in other years, in spite of its remoteness, is now a
ghastly desolation twenty-five miles long. Lying nearly
forty miles west of Grande Isle, it was nevertheless far
more populated a generation ago: it was not only the
most celebrated island of the group, but also the most
fashionable watering-place of the aristocratic South;—
to-day it is visited by fishermen only, at long intervals.
Its admirable beach in many respects resembled that of
Grande Isle to-day; the accommodations also were
much similar, although finer: a charming village of cottages facing the Gulf near the western end. The hotel
itself was a massive two-story construction of timber,
containing many apartments, together with a large din-
ing-room and dancing-hall. In rear of the hotel was a
bayou, where passengers landed—"Village Bayou" it is
still called by seamen;—but the deep channel which
now cuts the island in two a little eastwardly did not

exist while the village remained. The sea tore it out in one night—the same night when trees, fields, dwellings, all vanished into the Gulf, leaving no vestige of former human habitation except a few of those strong brick props and foundations upon which the frame houses and cisterns had been raised. One living creature was found there after the cataclysm—a cow! But how that solitary cow survived the fury of a storm-flood that actually rent the island in twain has ever remained a mystery. . . .

III.

On the Gulf side of these islands you may observe that the trees—when there are any trees—all bend away from the sea; and, even of bright, hot days when the wind sleeps, there is something grotesquely pathetic in their look of agonized terror. A group of oaks at Grande Isle I remember as especially suggestive: five stooping silhouettes in line against the horizon, like fleeing women with streaming garments and wind-blown hair,—bowing grievously and thrusting out arms desperately northward as to save themselves from falling. And they are being pursued indeed;—for the sea is devouring the land. Many and many a mile of ground has yielded to the tireless charging of Ocean's cavalry: far out you can see, through a good glass, the porpoises at play where of old the sugar-cane shook out its million bannerets; and shark-fins now seam deep water above a site where pigeons used to coo. Men build dikes; but the besieging tides bring up their bat-tering-rams—whole forests of drift—huge trunks of water-oak and weighty cypress. Forever the yellow Mis-sissippi strives to build; forever the sea struggles to destroy;—and amid their eternal strife the islands and the promontories change shape, more slowly, but not less fantastically, than the clouds of heaven.

And worthy of study are those wan battle-grounds where the woods made their last brave stand against the irresistible invasion,—usually at some long point of sea-marsh, widely fringed with billowing sand. Just where the waves curl beyond such a point you may dis-cern a multitude of blackened, snaggy shapes protrud-ing above the water,—some high enough to resemble ruined chimneys, others bearing a startling likeness to enormous skeleton-feet and skeleton-hands,—with crustaceous white growths clinging to them here and there like remnants of integument. These are bodies and limbs of drowned oaks,—so long drowned that the shell-scurf is inch-thick upon parts of them. Farther in upon the beach immense trunks lie overthrown. Some look like vast broken columns; some suggest colossal torsos imbedded, and seem to reach out mutilated stumps in despair from their deepening graves;—and beside these are others which have kept their feet with astounding obstinacy, although the barbarian tides have been charging them for twenty years, and gradu-ally torn away the soil above and beneath their roots. The sand around,—soft beneath and thinly crusted upon the surface,—is everywhere pierced with holes made by a beautifully mottled and semi-diaphanous crab, with hairy legs, big staring eyes, and milk-white claws;—while in the green sedges beyond there is a perpetual rustling, as of some strong wind beating among reeds: a marvellous creeping of "fiddlers," which the inexperienced visitor might at first mistake for so many peculiar beetles, as they run about sideways, each with his huge single claw folded upon his body like a wing-case. Year by year that rustling strip of green land grows narrower; the sand spreads and sinks, shuddering and wrinkling like a living brown skin; and the last standing corpses of the oaks, ever clinging with naked, dead feet to the sliding beach, lean more and more out of the perpendicular. As the sands subside, the stumps appear to creep; their intertwisted masses of snakish roots seem to crawl, to writhe,—like the reaching arms of cephalopods. . . .

. . . Grande Terre is going: the sea mines her fort, and will before many years carry the ramparts by storm. Grande Isle is going,—slowly but surely: the Gulf has eaten three miles into her meadowed land. Last Island has gone! How it went I first heard from the lips of a veteran pilot, while we sat one evening together on the trunk of a drifted cypress which some high tide had pressed deeply into the Grande Isle beach. The day had been tropically warm; we had sought the shore for a breath of living air. Sunset came, and with it the ponderous heat lifted,—a sudden breeze blew,—lightnings flickered in the darkening horizon,—wind and water began to strive together,—and soon all the low coast boomed. Then my companion began his story; perhaps the coming of the storm inspired him to speak! And as I listened to him, listening also to the clamoring of the coast, there flashed back to me recollection of a singular Breton fancy: that the Voice of the Sea is never one voice, but a tumult of many voices—voices of drowned men,—the muttering of multitudinous dead,—the moaning of innumerable ghosts, all rising, to rage against the living, at the great Witch call of storms. . . .

IV.

The charm of a single summer day on these island shores is something impossible to express, never to be forgotten. Rarely, in the paler zones, do earth and heaven take such luminosity: those will best understand me who have seen the splendor of a West Indian sky. And yet there is a tenderness of tint, a caress of color, in these Gulf-days which is not of the Antilles,—a spirituality, as of eternal tropical spring. It must have been to even such a sky that Xenophanes lifted up his eyes of old when he vowed the Infinite Blue was God;—it was indeed under such a sky that De Soto named the vastest and grandest of Southern havens Espiritu Santo,—the Bay of the Holy Ghost. There is a something unutterable in this bright Gulf-air that compels awe,—something vital, something holy, something pantheistic: and reverentially the mind asks itself if what the eye beholds is not the Pneuma indeed, the Infinite Breath, the Divine Ghost, the great Blue Soul of the Unknown. All, all is blue in the calm,—save the low land under your feet, which you almost forget, since it seems only as a tiny green flake afloat in the liquid eternity of day. Then slowly, caressingly, irresistibly, the witchery of the Infinite grows upon you: out of Time and Space you begin to dream with open eyes,—to drift into delicious oblivion of facts,—to forget the past, the present, the substantial,—to comprehend nothing but the existence of that infinite Blue Ghost as something into which you would wish to melt utterly away forever. . . .

And this day-magic of azure endures sometimes for months together. Cloudlessly the dawn reddens up through a violet east: there is no speck upon the blossoming of its Mystical Rose,—unless it be the silhouette of some passing gull, whirling his sickle-wings against the crimsoning. Ever, as the sun floats higher, the flood shifts its color. Sometimes smooth and gray, yet flickering with the morning gold, it is the vision of John,—the apocalyptic Sea of Glass mixed with fire;—again, with the growing breeze, it takes that incredible purple tint familiar mostly to painters of West Indian scenery;—once more, under the blaze of noon, it changes to a waste of broken emerald. With evening, the horizon assumes tints of inexpressible sweetness,—pearl-lights, opaline colors of milk and fire; and in the west are topaz-glowings and wondrous flushings as of nacre. Then, if the sea sleeps, it dreams of all these,—faintly, weirdly,—shadowing them even to the verge of heaven.

Beautiful, too, are those white phantasmagoria which, at the approach of equinoctial days, mark the coming of the winds. Over the rim of the sea a bright cloud gently pushes up its head. It rises; and others rise with it, to right and left—slowly at first; then more swiftly. All are brilliantly white and flocculent, like loose new cotton. Gradually they mount in enormous line high above the Gulf, rolling and wreathing into an arch that expands and advances,—bending from horizon to horizon. A clear, cold breath accompanies its coming. Reaching the zenith, it seems there to hang poised awhile,—a ghostly bridge arching the empyrean,—upreaching its measureless span from either underside of the world. Then the colossal phantom begins to turn, as on a pivot of air,—always preserving its curvilinear symmetry, but moving its unseen ends beyond and below the sky-circle. And at last it floats away unbroken beyond the blue sweep of the world, with a wind following after. Day after day, almost at the same hour, the white arc rises, wheels, and passes. . . .

. . . Never a glimpse of rock on these low shores;—only long sloping beaches and bars of smooth tawny sand. Sand and sea teem with vitality;—over all the dunes there is a constant susurration, a blattering and swarming of crustacea;—through all the sea there is a ceaseless play of silver lightning,—flashing of myriad fish. Sometimes the shallows are thickened with minute, transparent, crab-like organisms,—all colorless as gelatine. There are days also when countless medusæ drift in—beautiful veined creatures that throb like hearts, with perpetual systole and diastole of their diaphanous envelops: some, of translucent azure or rose, seem in the flood the shadows or ghosts of huge campanulate flowers;—others have the semblance of strange living vegetables,—great milky tubers, just beginning to sprout. But woe to the human skin grazed by those shadowy sproutings and spectral stamens!— the touch of glowing iron is not more painful. . . . Within an hour or two after their appearance all these tremulous jellies vanish mysteriously as they came.

Perhaps, if a bold swimmer, you may venture out alone a long way—once! Not twice!—even in company. As the water deepens beneath you, and you feel those ascending wave-currents of coldness arising which bespeak profundity, you will also begin to feel innumerable touches, as of groping fingers—touches of the bodies of fish, innumerable fish, fleeing towards shore. The farther you advance, the more thickly you will feel them come; and above you and around you, to right and left, others will leap and fall so swiftly as to daze the sight, like intercrossing fountain-jets of fluid silver. The gulls fly lower about you, circling with sinister squeaking cries;—perhaps for an instant your feet touch in the deep something heavy, swift, lithe, that rushes past with a swirling shock. Then the fear of the Abyss, the vast and voiceless Nightmare of the Sea, will come upon you; the silent panic of all those opaline millions that flee glimmering by will enter into you also. . . .

From what do they flee thus perpetually? Is it from the giant sawfish or the ravening shark?—from the herds of the porpoises, or from the *grande-écaille*,[3]— that splendid monster whom no net may hold,—all

3. "the grand-scale"; the great serpent

helmed and armored in argent plate-mail?—or from
the hideous devil-fish[4] of the Gulf,—gigantic, flat-bod-
ied, black, with immense side-fins ever outspread like
the pinions of a bat,—the terror of luggermen, the
uprooter of anchors? From all these, perhaps, and from
other monsters likewise—goblin shapes evolved by
Nature as destroyers, as equilibrists, as counterchecks
to that prodigious fecundity, which, unhindered, would
thicken the deep into one measureless and waveless ferment of being. . . . But when there are many bathers
these perils are forgotten,—numbers give courage,—one
can abandon one's self, without fear of the invisible, to
the long, quivering, electrical caresses of the sea. . . .

V.

Thirty years ago, Last Island lay steeped in the enormous light of even such magical days. July was
dying;—for weeks no fleck of cloud had broken the
heaven's blue dream of eternity; winds held their
breath; slow wavelets caressed the bland brown beach
with a sound as of kisses and whispers. To one who
found himself alone, beyond the limits of the village
and beyond the hearing of its voices,—the vast
silence, the vast light, seemed full of weirdness. And
these hushes, these transparencies, do not always
inspire a causeless apprehension: they are omens
sometimes—omens of coming tempest. Nature,—

4. sting-ray

incomprehensible Sphinx!—before her mightiest bursts of rage, ever puts forth her divinest witchery, makes more manifest her awful beauty. . . .

But in that forgotten summer the witchery lasted many long days,—days born in rose-light, buried in gold. It was the height of the season. The long myrtle-shadowed village was thronged with its summer population;—the big hotel could hardly accommodate all its guests;—the bathing-houses were too few for the crowds who flocked to the water morning and evening. There were diversions for all,—hunting and fishing parties, yachting excursions, rides, music, games, promenades. Carriage wheels whirled flickering along the beach, seaming its smoothness noiselessly, as if muffled. Love wrote its dreams upon the sand. . . .

. . . Then one great noon, when the blue abyss of day seemed to yawn over the world more deeply than ever before, a sudden change touched the quicksilver smoothness of the waters—the swaying shadow of a vast motion. First the whole sea-circle appeared to rise up bodily at the sky; the horizon-curve lifted to a straight line; the line darkened and approached,—a monstrous wrinkle, an immeasurable fold of green water, moving swift as a cloud-shadow pursued by sunlight. But it had looked formidable only by startling contrast with the previous placidity of the open: it was scarcely two feet high;—it curled slowly as it neared the beach, and combed itself out in sheets of woolly foam with a low, rich roll of whispered thunder. Swift in pursuit another followed—a third—a feebler fourth; then the sea only swayed a little, and stilled again. Minutes

passed, and the immeasurable heaving recom-
menced—one, two, three, four . . . seven long swells
this time;—and the Gulf smoothed itself once more.
Irregularly the phenomenon continued to repeat itself,
each time with heavier billowing and briefer intervals
of quiet—until at last the whole sea grew restless and
shifted color and flickered green;—the swells became
shorter and changed form. Then from horizon to shore
ran one uninterrupted heaving—one vast green
swarming of snaky shapes, rolling in to hiss and flatten
upon the sand. Yet no single cirrus-speck revealed itself
through all the violet heights: there was no wind!—you
might have fancied the sea had been upheaved from
beneath. . . .

And indeed the fancy of a seismic origin for a wind-
less surge would not appear in these latitudes to be
utterly without foundation. On the fairest days a
southeast breeze may bear you an odor singular enough
to startle you from sleep,—a strong, sharp smell as of
fish-oil; and gazing at the sea you might be still more
startled at the sudden apparition of great oleaginous
patches spreading over the water, sheeting over the
swells. That is, if you had never heard of the mysterious submarine oil-wells, the volcanic fountains, unex-
plored, that well up with the eternal pulsing of the
Gulf-Stream. . . .

But the pleasure-seekers of Last Island knew there
must have been a "great blow" somewhere that day.
Still the sea swelled; and a splendid surf made the
evening bath delightful. Then, just at sundown, a
beautiful cloud-bridge grew up and arched the sky

with a single span of cottony pink vapor, that changed
and deepened color with the dying of the iridescent
day. And the cloud-bridge approached, stretched,
strained, and swung round at last to make way for the
coming of the gale,—even as the light bridges that tra-
verse the dreamy Têche swing open when luggermen
sound through their conch-shells the long, bellowing
signal of approach.

Then the wind began to blow, with the passing of
July. It blew from the northeast, clear, cool. It blew in
enormous sighs, dying away at regular intervals, as if
pausing to draw breath. All night it blew; and in each
pause could be heard the answering moan of the rising
surf,—as if the rhythm of the sea moulded itself after
the rhythm of the air,—as if the waving of the water
responded precisely to the waving of the wind,—a billow for every puff, a surge for every sigh.

The August morning broke in a bright sky;—the
breeze still came cool and clear from the northeast.
The waves were running now at a sharp angle to the
shore: they began to carry fleeces, an innumerable
flock of vague green shapes, wind-driven to be
despoiled of their ghostly wool. Far as the eye could
follow the line of the beach, all the slope was white
with the great shearing of them. Clouds came, flew as
in a panic against the face of the sun, and passed. All
that day and through the night and into the morning
again the breeze continued from the northeast, blowing like an equinoctial gale. . . .

Then day by day the vast breath freshened steadily,
and the waters heightened. A week later sea-bathing

had become perilous: colossal breakers were herding in, like moving leviathan-backs, twice the height of a man. Still the gale grew, and the billowing waxed mightier, and faster and faster overhead flew the tatters of torn cloud. The gray morning of the 9th wanly lighted a surf that appalled the best swimmers: the sea was one wild agony of foam, the gale was rending off the heads of the waves and veiling the horizon with a fog of salt spray. Shadowless and gray the day remained; there were mad bursts of lashing rain. Evening brought with it a sinister apparition, looming through a cloud-rent in the west—a scarlet sun in a green sky. His sanguine disk, enormously magnified, seemed barred like the body of a belted planet. A moment, and the crimson spectre vanished; and the moonless night came.

Then the Wind grew weird. It ceased being a breath; it became a Voice moaning across the world,—hooting,—uttering nightmare sounds,—*Whoo!—whoo!—whoo!*—and with each stupendous owl-cry the mooing of the waters seemed to deepen, more and more abysmally, through all the hours of darkness. From the northwest the breakers of the bay began to roll high over the sandy slope, into the salines;—the village bayou broadened to a bellowing flood. . . . So the tumult swelled and the turmoil heightened until morning,—a morning of gray gloom and whistling rain. Rain of bursting clouds and rain of wind-blown brine from the great spuming agony of the sea.

The steamer *Star* was due from St. Mary's that fearful morning. Could she come? No one really believed it,—no one. And nevertheless men struggled to the roaring beach to look for her, because hope is stronger than reason. . . .

Even to-day, in these Creole islands, the advent of the steamer is the great event of the week. There are no telegraph lines, no telephones: the mail-packet is the only trustworthy medium of communication with the outer world, bringing friends, news, letters. The magic of steam has placed New Orleans nearer to New York than to the Timbaliers, nearer to Washington than to Wine Island, nearer to Chicago than to Barataria Bay. And even during the deepest sleep of waves and winds there will come betimes to sojourners in this unfamiliar archipelago a feeling of lonesomeness that is a fear, a feeling of isolation from the world of men,—totally unlike that sense of solitude which haunts one in the silence of mountain-heights, or amid the eternal tumult of lofty granitic coasts: a sense of helpless insecurity. The land seems but an undulation of the seabed: its highest ridges do not rise more than the height of a man above the salines on either side;—the salines themselves lie almost level with the level of the floodtides;—the tides are variable, treacherous, mysterious. But when all around and above these ever-changing shores the twin vastnesses of heaven and sea begin to utter the tremendous revelation of themselves as infinite forces in contention, then indeed this sense of separation from humanity appals. . . . Perhaps it was such a feeling which forced men, on the tenth day of August, eighteen hundred and fifty-six, to hope against hope for the coming of the *Star*, and to strain their eyes towards far-off Terrebonne. "It was a wind you could lie down on," said my friend the pilot.

. . . "Great God!" shrieked a voice above the shouting of the storm,—"*she is coming!*" . . . It was true. Down the Atchafalaya, and thence through strange mazes of bayou, lakelet, and pass, by a rear route familiar only to the best of pilots, the frail river-craft had toiled into Caillou Bay, running close to the main shore;—and now she was heading right for the island, with the wind aft, over the monstrous sea. On she came, swaying, rocking, plunging,—with a great whiteness wrapping her about like a cloud, and moving with her moving,—a tempest-whirl of spray;—ghost-white and like a ghost she came, for her smoke-stacks exhaled no visible smoke—the wind devoured it! The excitement on shore became wild;—men shouted themselves hoarse; women laughed and cried. Every telescope and opera-glass was directed upon the coming apparition; all wondered how the pilot kept his feet; all marvelled at the madness of the captain.

But Captain Abraham Smith was not mad. A veteran American sailor, he had learned to know the great Gulf as scholars know deep books by heart: he knew the birthplace of its tempests, the mystery of its tides, the omens of its hurricanes. While lying at Brashear City he felt the storm had not yet reached its highest, vaguely foresaw a mighty peril, and resolved to wait no longer for a lull. "Boys," he said, "we've got to take her out in spite of Hell!" And they "took her out." Through all the peril, his men stayed by him and obeyed him. By mid-morning the wind had deepened to a roar,—lowering sometimes to a rumble, sometimes bursting upon the ears like a measureless and deafening crash. Then the captain knew the *Star* was running a race with Death. "She'll win it," he muttered;—"she'll stand it. . . . Perhaps they'll have need of me to-night."

She won! With a sonorous steam-chant of triumph the brave little vessel rode at last into the bayou, and anchored hard by her accustomed resting-place, in full view of the hotel, though not near enough to shore to lower her gang-plank. . . . But she had sung her swan-song. Gathering in from the northeast, the waters of the bay were already marbling over the salines and half across the island; and still the wind increased its paroxysmal power.

Cottages began to rock. Some slid away from the solid props upon which they rested. A chimney tumbled. Shutters were wrenched off; verandas demolished. Light roofs lifted, dropped again, and flapped into ruin. Trees bent their heads to the earth. And still the storm grew louder and blacker with every passing hour.

The *Star* rose with the rising of the waters, dragging her anchor. Two more anchors were put out, and still she dragged—dragged in with the flood,—twisting, shuddering, careening in her agony. Evening fell; the sand began to move with the wind, stinging faces like a continuous fire of fine shot; and frenzied blasts came to buffet the steamer forward, sideward. Then one of her hog-chains parted with a clang like the boom of a big bell. Then another! . . . Then the captain bade his men to cut away all her upper works, clean to the deck. Overboard into the seething went her stacks, her pilot-house, her cabins,—and whirled away. And the naked hull of the *Star*, still dragging her three anchors, labored on through the darkness, nearer and nearer to the immense silhouette of the hotel, whose hundred windows were now all aflame. The vast timber building seemed to defy the storm. The wind, roaring round its broad verandas,—hissing through every crevice with the sound and force of steam,—appeared to waste its rage. And in the half-lull between two terrible gusts there came to the captain's ears a sound that seemed strange in that night of multitudinous terrors . . . a sound of music!

VI.

. . . Almost every evening throughout the season there had been dancing in the great hall;—there was dancing that night also. The population of the hotel had been augmented by the advent of families from other parts of the island, who found their summer cottages insecure places of shelter: there were nearly four hundred guests assembled. Perhaps it was for this reason that the entertainment had been prepared upon a grander plan than usual, that it assumed the form of a fashionable ball. And all those pleasure-seekers,—representing the wealth and beauty of the Creole parishes,—whether from Ascension or Assumption, St. Mary's or St. Landry's, Iberville or Terrebonne, whether inhabitants

of the multi-colored and many-balconied Creole quarter of the quaint metropolis, or dwellers in the dreamy
paradises of the Têche,—mingled joyously, knowing
each other, feeling in some sort akin—whether affili-
ated by blood, connaturalized by caste, or simply
interassociated by traditional sympaties of class sentiment and class interest. Perhaps in the more than ordinary merriment of that evening something of nervous
exaltation might have been discerned,—something like
a feverish resolve to oppose apprehension with gayety,
to combat uneasiness by diversion. But the hours
passed in mirthfulness; the first general feeling of
depression began to weigh less and less upon the
guests; they had found reason to confide in the solidity
of the massive building; there were no positive terrors,
no outspoken fears; and the new conviction of all had
found expression in the words of the host himself,—"*Il
n'y a rien de mieux à faire que de s'amuser!*" Of what
avail to lament the prospective devastation of cane-
fields,—to discuss the possible ruin of crops? Better to
seek solace in choregraphic harmonies, in the rhythm
of gracious motion and of perfect melody, than
hearken to the discords of the wild orchestra of
storms;—wiser to admire the grace of Parisian toilets,
the eddy of trailing robes with its fairy-foam of lace,
the ivorine loveliness of glossy shoulders and jewelled
throats, the glimmering of satin-slippered feet,—than
to watch the raging of the flood without, or the flying
of the wrack. . . .

So the music and the mirth went on: they made joy
for themselves—those elegant guests;—they jested and

sipped rich wines;—they pledged, and hoped, and loved, and promised, with never a thought of the morrow, on the night of the tenth of August, eighteen hundred and fifty-six. Observant parents were there, planning for the future bliss of their nearest and dearest;—mothers and fathers of handsome lads, lithe and elegant as young pines, and fresh from the polish of foreign university training;—mothers and fathers of splendid girls whose simplest attitudes were witcheries. Young cheeks flushed, young hearts fluttered with an emotion more puissant than the excitement of the dance;—young eyes betrayed the happy secret discreeter lips would have preserved. Slave-servants circled through the aristocratic press, bearing dainties and wines, praying permission to pass in terms at once humble and officious,—always in the excellent French which well-trained house-servants were taught to use on such occasions.

. . . Night wore on: still the shining floor palpitated to the feet of the dancers; still the piano-forte pealed, and still the violins sang,—and the sound of their singing shrilled through the darkness, in gasps of the gale, to the ears of Captain Smith, as he strove to keep his footing on the spray-drenched deck of the *Star*.

—"Christ!" he muttered,—"a dance! If that wind whips round south, there'll be another dance! . . . But I guess the *Star* will stay." . . .

Half an hour might have passed; still the lights flamed calmly, and the violins trilled, and the perfumed whirl went on. . . . And suddenly the wind veered!

Again the *Star* reeled, and shuddered, and turned, and began to drag all her anchors. But she now dragged away from the great building and its lights,—away from the voluptuous thunder of the grand piano,— even at that moment outpouring the great joy of Weber's melody orchestrated by Berlioz: *l'Invitation à la Valse*,—with its marvellous musical swing!

—"Waltzing!" cried the captain. "God help them!— God help us all now! . . . *The Wind waltzes to-night, with the Sea for his partner!*" . . .

O the stupendous Valse-Tourbillon! O the mighty Dancer! One—two—three! From northeast to east, from east to southeast, from southeast to south: then from the south he came, whirling the Sea in his arms. . . .

. . . Some one shrieked in the midst of the revels;— some girl who found her pretty slippers wet. What could it be? Thin streams of water were spreading over the level planking,—curling about the feet of the dancers. . . . What could it be? All the land had begun to quake, even as, but a moment before, the polished floor was trembling to the pressure of circling steps;— all the building shook now; every beam uttered its groan. What could it be? . . .

There was a clamor, a panic, a rush to the windy night. Infinite darkness above and beyond; but the lantern-beams danced far out over an unbroken circle of heaving and swirling black water. Stealthily, swiftly, the measureless sea-flood was rising.

—"*Messieurs—mesdames, ce n'est rien.* Nothing seri- ous, ladies, I assure you. . . . *Mais nous en avons vu bien souvent, les inondations comme celle-ci; ça passe vite!* The water will go down in a few hours, ladies;—it never rises higher than this; *il n'y a pas le moindre danger, je vous dis! Allons! il n'y a*—My God! what is that?" . . .

For a moment there was a ghastly hush of voices. And through that hush there burst upon the ears of all a fearful and unfamiliar sound, as of a colossal cannonade—rolling up from the south, with volleying lightnings. Vastly and swiftly, nearer and nearer it came,—a ponderous and unbroken thunder-roll, terrible as the long muttering of an earthquake.

The nearest mainland,—across mad Caillou Bay to the sea-marshes,—lay twelve miles north; west, by the Gulf, the nearest solid ground was twenty miles distant. There were boats, yes!—but the stoutest swimmer might never reach them now! . . .

Then rose a frightful cry,—the hoarse, hideous, indescribable cry of hopeless fear,—the despairing animal-cry man utters when suddenly brought face to face with Nothingness, without preparation, without consolation, without possibility of respite. . . . *Sauve qui peut!*[5] Some wrenched down the doors; some clung to the heavy banquet-tables, to the sofas, to the billiard-tables:—during one terrible instant,—against fruitless heroisms, against futile generosities,—raged all the frenzy of selfishness, all the brutalities of panic. And then—then came, thundering through the blackness, the giant swells, boom on boom! . . . One crash!—the huge frame building rocks like a cradle, seesaws, crackles. What are human shrieks now?—the tornado is

5. Save what floats!

shrieking! Another!—chandeliers splinter; lights are
dashed out; a sweeping cataract hurls in: the immense
hall rises,—oscillates,—twirls as upon a pivot,—crepi-
tates,—crumbles into ruin. Crash again!—the swirling
wreck dissolves into the wallowing of another monster
billow; and a hundred cottages overturn, spin in sudden eddies, quiver, disjoint, and melt into the seething.

. . . So the hurricane passed,—tearing off the heads
of the prodigious waves, to hurl them a hundred feet in
air,—heaping up the ocean against the land,—upturning the woods. Bays and passes were swollen to abysses;
rivers regorged; the sea-marshes were changed to raging
wastes of water. Before New Orleans the flood of the
mile-broad Mississippi rose six feet above highest water-
mark. One hundred and ten miles away, Donaldsonville
trembled at the towering tide of the Lafourche. Lakes
strove to burst their boundaries. Far-off river steamers
tugged wildly at their cables,—shivering like tethered
creatures that hear by night the approaching howl of
destroyers. Smoke-stacks were hurled overboard, pilot-
houses torn away, cabins blown to fragments.

And over roaring Kaimbuck Pass,—over the agony
of Caillou Bay,—the billowing tide rushed unresisted
from the Gulf,—tearing and swallowing the land in its
course,—ploughing out deep-sea channels where sleek
herds had been grazing but a few hours before,—rending islands in twain,—and ever bearing with it,
through the night, enormous vortex of wreck and vast
wan drift of corpses. . . .

But the *Star* remained. And Captain Abraham
Smith, with a long, good rope about his waist, dashed

again and again into that awful surging to snatch victims from death,—clutching at passing hands, heads, garments, in the cataract-sweep of the seas,—saving, aiding, cheering, though blinded by spray and battered by drifting wreck, until his strength failed in the unequal struggle at last, and his men drew him aboard senseless, with some beautiful half-drowned girl safe in his arms. But well-nigh twoscore souls had been rescued by him; and the *Star* stayed on through it all.

Long years after, the weed-grown ribs of her graceful skeleton could still be seen, curving up from the sand-dunes of Last Island, in valiant witness of how well she stayed.

VII.

Day breaks through the flying wrack, over the infinite heaving of the sea, over the low land made vast with desolation. It is a spectral dawn: a wan light, like the light of a dying sun.

The wind has waned and veered; the flood sinks slowly back to its abysses—abandoning its plunder,— scattering its piteous waifs over bar and dune, over shoal and marsh, among the silences of the mango-swamps,[6] over the long low reaches of sand-grasses and drowned weeds, for more than a hundred miles. From the shell-reefs of Pointe-au-Fer to the shallows of Pelto

---

6. Hearn probably intended this to be "mangrove-swamp." The mangrove is a land-building tropical shrub with gnarled aerial roots found in brackish swamps of the Gulf of Mexico and along inland side of barrier islands.

Bay the dead lie mingled with the high-heaped drift;— from their cypress groves the vultures rise to dispute a share of the feast with the shrieking frigate-birds and squeaking gulls. And as the tremendous tide withdraws its plunging waters, all the pirates of air follow the great white-gleaming retreat: a storm of billowing wings and screaming throats.

And swift in the wake of gull and frigate-bird the Wreckers come, the Spoilers of the dead,—savage skimmers of the sea,—hurricane-riders wont to spread their canvas-pinions in the face of storms; Sicilian and Corsican outlaws, Manila-men from the marshes, deserters from many navies, Lascars, marooners,[7] refugees of a hundred nationalities,—fishers and shrimpers by name, smugglers by opportunity,—wild channel-finders from obscure bayous and unfamiliar *chênières*, all skilled in the mysteries of these mysterious waters beyond the comprehension of the oldest licensed pilot. . . .

There is plunder for all—birds and men. There are drowned sheep in multitude, heaped carcasses of kine. There are casks of claret and kegs of brandy and legions of bottles bobbing in the surf. There are billiard-tables overturned upon the sand;—there are sofas, pianos, footstools and music-stools, luxurious chairs, lounges of bamboo. There are chests of cedar, and toilet-tables of rosewood, and trunks of fine stamped leather stored with precious apparel. There are *objets de luxe* innumerable. There are children's playthings: French dolls in marvellous toilets, and toy carts, and wooden horses,

7. escaped slaves who hid in the remote wilderness areas of the coastal swamps of south Louisiana

and wooden spades, and brave little wooden ships that rode out the gale in which the great *Nautilus* went down. There is money in notes and in coin—in purses, in pocketbooks, and in pockets: plenty of it! There are silks, satins, laces, and fine linen to be stripped from the bodies of the drowned,—and necklaces, bracelets, watches, finger-rings and fine chains, brooches and trinkets. . . . "*Chi bidizza!—Oh! chi bedda mughieri! Eccu, la bidizza!*" That ball-dress was made in Paris by—But you never heard of him, Sicilian Vicenzu. . . . "*Che bella sposina!*" Her betrothal ring will not come off, Giuseppe; but the delicate bone snaps easily: your oyster-knife can sever the tendon. . . . "*Guardate! chi bedda picciota!*" Over her heart you will find it, Valentino—the locket held by that fine Swiss chain of woven hair—"*Caya manan!*" And it is not your quadroon bondsmaid, sweet lady, who now disrobes you so roughly; those Malay hands are less deft than hers,—but she slumbers very far away from you, and may not be aroused from her sleep. "*Na quita mo! dalaga!—na quita maganda!*" . . . Juan, the fastenings of those diamond ear-drops are much too complicated for your peon fingers: tear them out!—"*Dispense, chulita!*" . . .

. . . Suddenly a long, mighty silver trilling fills the ears of all: there is a wild hurrying and scurrying; swiftly, one after another, the overburdened luggers spread wings and flutter away.

Thrice the great cry rings rippling through the gray air, and over the green sea, and over the far-flooded shell-reefs, where the huge white flashes are,—sheet-lightning of breakers,—and over the weird wash of corpses coming in.

It is the steam-call of the relief-boat, hastening to rescue the living, to gather in the dead.

The tremendous tragedy is over!

Part II

OUT OF THE SEA'S STRENGTH

I.

There are regions of Louisiana coast whose aspect seems not of the present, but of the immemorial past— of that epoch when low flat reaches of primordial continent first rose into form above a Silurian sea. To indulge this geologic dream, any fervid and breezeless day there, it is only necessary to ignore the evolutional protests of a few blue asters or a few composite flowers of the *caryopsis* sort, which contrive to display their rare flashes of color through the general waving of cat-heads, blood-weeds, wild cane, and marsh grasses. For, at a hasty glance, the general appearance of this marsh verdure is vague enough, as it ranges away towards the sand, to convey the idea of amphibious vegetation,—a primitive flora as yet undecided whether to retain marine habits and forms, or to assume terrestrial ones;—and the occasional inspection of surprising shapes might strengthen this fancy. Queer flat-lying and many-branching things, which resemble sea-weeds in juiciness and color and consistency, crackle under your feet from time to time; the moist and weighty air seems heated rather from below than from above,—less by the sun than by the radiation of a cooling world; and the mists of morning or evening appear to simulate the vapory exhalation of volcanic forces,—latent, but only dozing, and uncomfortably close to the surface. And indeed geologists have actually averred that those rare elevations of the soil,—which, with their heavy coronets of evergreen foliage, not only look like islands, but are so called in the French nomenclature of the coast,—have been prominences created by ancient mud volcanoes.

The family of a Spanish fisherman, Feliu Viosca, once occupied and gave its name to such an islet, quite close to the Gulf-shore,—the loftiest bit of land along fourteen miles of just such marshy coast as I have spoken of. Landward, it dominated a desolation that wearied the eye to look at, a wilderness of reedy sloughs, patched at intervals with ranges of bitter-weed, tufts of elbow-bushes, and broad reaches of saw-grass, stretching away to a bluish-green line of woods that closed the horizon, and imperfectly drained in the driest season by a slimy little bayou that continually vomited foul water into the sea. The point had been much discussed by geologists; it proved a godsend to United States surveyors weary of attempting to take observations among quagmires, moccasins, and arborescent weeds from fifteen to twenty feet high. Savage fishermen, at some unrecorded time, had heaped upon the eminence a hill of clam-shells,—refuse of a million feasts; earth again had been formed over these, perhaps by the blind agency of worms working through centuries unnumbered; and the new soil had given birth to a luxuriant vegetation. Millennial oaks interknotted their roots below its surface, and vouchsafed protection to many a frailer growth of shrub or tree,—wild orange, water-willow, palmetto, locust, pomegranate, and many trailing tendrilled things, both green and gray. Then,—perhaps about half a century ago,—a few white fishermen cleared a place for themselves in this grove, and built a few palmetto cottages, with boat-houses and a wharf, facing the bayou. Later on this temporary fishing station became a permanent settlement: homes constructed of heavy timber and plaster mixed with the trailing moss of the oaks and cypresses took the places of the frail and fragrant huts of palmetto. Still the population itself retained a floating character: it ebbed and came, according to season and circumstances, according to luck or loss in the tilling of the sea. Viosca, the founder of the settlement, always remained; he always managed to do well. He owned several luggers and sloops, which were hired out upon excellent terms; he could make large and profitable contracts with New Orleans fish-dealers; and he was vaguely suspected of possessing more occult resources. There were some confused stories current about his having once been a daring smuggler, and having only been reformed by the pleadings of his wife Carmen,—a little brown woman who had followed him from Barcelona to share his fortunes in the western world.

On hot days, when the shade was full of thin sweet scents, the place had a tropical charm, a drowsy peace. Nothing except the peculiar appearance of the line of oaks facing the Gulf could have conveyed to the visitor any suggestion of days in which the trilling of crickets and the fluting of birds had ceased, of nights when the voices of the marsh had been hushed for fear. In one enormous rank the veteran trees stood shoulder to shoulder, but in the attitude of giants over-mastered,—forced backward towards the marsh,—made to recoil by the might of the ghostly enemy with whom they had striven a thousand years,—the Shrieker, the Sky-Sweeper, the awful Sea-Wind!

Never had he given them so terrible a wrestle as on the night of the tenth of August, eighteen hundred and fifty-six. All the waves of the excited Gulf thronged in as if to see, and lifted up their voices, and pushed, and roared, until the *chênière* was islanded by such a billowing as no white man's eyes had ever looked upon before. Grandly the oaks bore themselves, but every fibre of their knotted thews was strained in the unequal contest, and two of the giants were overthrown, upturning, as they fell, roots coiled and huge as the serpent-limbs of Titans. Moved to its entrails, all the islet trembled, while the sea magnified its menace, and reached out whitely to the prostrate trees; but the rest of the oaks stood on, and strove in line, and saved the habitations defended by them. . . .

II.

Before a little waxen image of the Mother and Child,— an odd little Virgin with an Indian face, brought home by Feliu as a gift after one of his Mexican voyages,— Carmen Viosca had burned candles and prayed; sometimes telling her beads; sometimes murmuring the litanies she knew by heart; sometimes also reading from a prayer-book worn and greasy as a long-used pack of cards. It was particularly stained at one page, a page on which her tears had fallen many a lonely night—a page with a clumsy wood-cut representing a celestial lamp, a symbolic radiance, shining through darkness, and on either side a kneeling angel with folded wings. And beneath this rudely wrought symbol of the Perpetual Calm appeared in big, coarse type the title of a prayer that has been offered up through many a century, doubtless, by wives of Spanish mariners,—*Contra las Tempestades.*

Once she became very much frightened. After a partial lull the storm had suddenly redoubled its force: the ground shook; the house quivered and creaked; the wind brayed and screamed and pushed and scuffled at the door; and the water, which had been whipping in through every crevice, all at once rose over the threshold and flooded the dwelling. Carmen dipped her finger in the water and tasted it. It was salt!

And none of Feliu's boats had yet come in;—doubt-less they had been driven into some far-away bayous by the storm. The only boat at the settlement, the *Car-mencita*, had been almost wrecked by running upon a snag three days before;—there was at least a fortnight's work for the ship-carpenter of Dead Cypress Point. And Feliu was sleeping as if nothing unusual had hap-pened—the heavy sleep of a sailor, heedless of commo-tions and voices. And his men, Miguel and Mateo, were at the other end of the *chênière*.

With a scream Carmen aroused Feliu. He raised himself upon his elbow, rubbed his eyes, and asked her, with exasperating calmness, "*¿Qué tienes? ¿qué tienes?*" (What ails thee?)

—"Oh, Feliu! the sea is coming upon us!" she answered, in the same tongue. But she screamed out a word inspired by her fear: she did not cry, "*¡Se nos viene el mar encima!*" but "*¡Se nos viene LA ALTURA!*"[8]—the name that conveys the terrible thought of depth swal-lowed up in height,—the height of the *high sea*.

"*¡No lo creo!*"[9] muttered Feliu, looking at the floor; then in a quiet, deep voice he said, pointing to an oar in the corner of the room, "*Echame ese remo.*"

She gave it to him. Still reclining upon one elbow, Feliu measured the depth of the water with his thumb-nail upon the blade of the oar, and then bade Carmen light his pipe for him. His calmness reassured her. For half an hour more, undismayed by the clam-oring of the wind or the calling of the sea, Feliu silently smoked his pipe and watched his oar. The

8. "The sea is coming over us!" . . . "THE HEIGHT is coming to us!"
9. "I don't think so!"

water rose a little higher, and he made another mark;—then it climbed a little more, but not so rapidly; and he smiled at Carmen as he made a third mark. "*¡Como creía!*" he exclaimed, "*no hay porque asustarse: ¡el agua baja!*"[10] And as Carmen would have continued to pray, he rebuked her fears, and bade her try to obtain some rest: "*¡Basta ya de plegarios, querida!—vete y duerme.*"[11] His tone, though kindly, was imperative; and Carmen, accustomed to obey him, laid herself down by his side, and soon, for very weariness, slept.

It was a feverish sleep, nevertheless, shattered at brief intervals by terrible sounds—sounds magnified by her nervous condition—a sleep visited by dreams that mingled in a strange way with the impressions of the storm, and more than once made her heart stop, and start again at its own stopping. One of these fancies she never could forget—a dream about little Concha,—Conchita, her firstborn, who now slept far away in the old churchyard at Barcelona. She had tried to become resigned,—not to think. But the child would come back night after night, though the earth lay heavy upon her—night after night, through long distances of Time and Space. Oh! the fancied clinging of infant-lips!—the thrilling touch of little ghostly hands!—those phantom-caresses that torture mothers' hearts! . . . Night after night, through many a month of pain. Then for a time the gentle presence ceased to haunt

---

10. "Like I thought . . . there's no reason to be frightened; the water's going down!"
11. "Enough prayers, dear!—stop worrying and go to sleep."

her,—seemed to have lain down to sleep forever under the high bright grass and yellow flowers. Why did it return, that night of all nights, to kiss her, to cling to her, to nestle in her arms? . . .

For in her dream she thought herself still kneeling before the waxen Image, while the terrors of the tempest were ever deepening about her,—raving of winds and booming of waters and a shaking of the land. And before her, even as she prayed her dream-prayer, the waxen Virgin became tall as a woman, and taller,—rising to the roof and smiling as she grew. Then Carmen would have cried out for fear, but that something smothered her voice,—paralyzed her tongue. And the Virgin silently stooped above her, and placed in her arms the Child,—the brown Child with the Indian face. And the Child whitened in her hands and changed,—seeming as it changed to send a sharp pain through her heart: an old pain linked somehow with memories of bright windy Spanish hills, and summer-scent of olive groves, and all the luminous Past;—it looked into her face with the soft dark gaze, with the unforgotten smile of . . . dead Conchita!

And Carmen wished to thank the smiling Virgin for that priceless bliss, and lifted up her eyes; but the sickness of ghostly fear returned upon her when she looked; for now the Mother seemed as a woman long dead, and the smile was the smile of fleshlessness, and the places of the eyes were voids and darknesses. . . . And the sea sent up so vast a roar that the dwelling rocked.

Carmen started from sleep to find her heart throbbing so that the couch shook with it. Night was growing gray; the door had just been opened and slammed again. Through the rain-whipped panes she discerned the passing shape of Feliu, making for the beach—a broad and bearded silhouette, bending against the wind. Still the waxen Virgin smiled her Mexican smile,—but now she was only seven inches high; and her bead-glass eyes seemed to twinkle with kindliness while the flame of the last expiring taper struggled for life in the earthen socket at her feet.

III.

Rain and a blind sky and a bursting sea. Feliu and his men, Miguel and Mateo, looked out upon the thundering and flashing of the monstrous tide. The wind had fallen, and the gray air was full of gulls. Behind the *chênière*, back to the cloudy line of low woods many miles away, stretched a wash of lead-colored water, with a green point piercing it here and there—elbow-bushes or wild cane tall enough to keep their heads above the flood. But the inundation was visibly decreasing;—with the passing of each hour more and more green patches and points had been showing themselves: by degrees the course of the bayou had become defined—two parallel winding lines of dwarf-timber and bushy shrubs traversing the water toward the distant cypress-swamps. Before the *chênière* all the shell-beach slope was piled with wreck—uptorn trees with the foliage still fresh upon them, splintered timbers of mysterious origin, and logs in multitude, scarred with gashes of the axe. Feliu and

his comrades had saved wood enough to build a little
town,—working up to their waists in the surf, with
ropes, poles, and boat-hooks. The whole sea was full of
flotsam. *¡Voto a Cristo!* [12]—what a wrecking there must
have been! And to think the *Carmencita* could not be
taken out!

They had seen other luggers making eastward during the morning—could recognize some by their sails,
others by their gait,—exaggerated in their struggle with
the pitching of the sea: the *San Pablo*, the *Gasparina*,
the *Enriqueta*, the *Agueda*, the *Constanza*. Ugly water,
yes!—but what a chance for wreckers! . . . Some great
ship must have gone to pieces;—scores of casks were
rolling in the trough,—casks of wine. Perhaps it was
the *Manila*,—perhaps the *Nautilus*!

A dead cow floated near enough for Mateo to throw
his rope over one horn; and they all helped to get it
out. It was a milch cow of some expensive breed; and
the owner's brand had been burned upon the horns:—
a monographic combination of the letters A and P.
Feliu said he knew that brand: Old-man Preaulx, of
Belle-Isle, who kept a sort of dairy at Last Island during the summer season, used to mark all his cows that
way. Strange!

But, as they worked on, they began to see stranger
things,—white dead faces and dead hands, which did
not look like the hands or the faces of drowned sailors:
the ebb was beginning to run strongly, and these were
passing out with it on the other side of the mouth of

12. Christ help them!

the bayou;—perhaps they had been washed into the marsh during the night, when the great rush of the sea came. Then the three men left the water, and retired to higher ground to scan the furrowed Gulf;—their practiced eyes began to search the courses of the sea-currents,—keen as the gaze of birds that watch the wake of the plough. And soon the casks and the drift were forgotten; for it seemed to them that the tide was heavy with human dead—passing out, processionally, to the great open. Very far, where the huge pitching of the swells was diminished by distance into a mere fluttering of ripples, the water appeared as if sprinkled with them;—they vanished and became visible again at irregular intervals, here and there—floating most thickly eastward,—tossing, swaying patches of white or pink or blue or black, each with its tiny speck of flesh-color showing as the sea lifted or lowered the body. Nearer to shore there were few; but of these two were close enough to be almost recognizable: Miguel first discerned them. They were rising and falling where the water was deepest—well out in front of the mouth of the bayou, beyond the flooded sand-bars, and moving toward the shell-reef westward. They were drifting almost side by side. One was that of a negro, apparently well attired, and wearing a white apron;—the other seemed to be a young colored girl, clad in a blue dress; she was floating upon her face; they could observe that she had nearly straight hair, braided and tied with a red ribbon. These were evidently house-servants,—slaves. But from whence? Nothing could be learned until the luggers should return; and none of them was yet in sight. Still Feliu was not anxious as to the fate of his boats, manned by the best sailors of the coast. Rarely are these Louisiana fishermen lost in sudden storms; even when to other eyes the appearances are most pacific and the skies most splendidly blue, they divine some far-off danger, like the gulls; and like the gulls also, you see their light vessels fleeing landward. These men seem living barometers, exquisitely sensitive to all the invisible changes of atmospheric expansion and compression; they are not easily caught in those awful dead calms which suddenly paralyze the wings of a bark, and hold her helpless in their charmed circle, as in a nightmare, until the blackness overtakes her, and the long-sleeping sea leaps up foaming to devour her.

—"¡Carajo!"[13]

The word all at once bursts from Feliu's mouth, with that peculiar guttural snarl of the "r" betokening strong excitement,—while he points to something rocking in the ebb, beyond the foaming of the shell-reef, under a circling of gulls. More dead? Yes—but something too that lives and moves, like a quivering speck of gold; and Mateo also perceives it, a gleam of bright hair,—and Miguel likewise, after a moment's gazing. A living child;—a lifeless mother. ¡Pobrecita![14] No boat within reach, and only a mighty surf-wrestler could hope to swim thither and return!

But already, without a word, brown Feliu has stripped for the struggle;—another second, and he is

13. [expletive]
14. "Poor little thing!"

shooting through the surf, head and hands tunnelling the foam hills. . . . One—two—three lines passed!—four!—that is where they first begin to crumble white from the summit,—five!—that he can ride fearlessly! . . . Then swiftly, easily, he advances, with a long, powerful breast-stroke,—keeping his bearded head well up to watch for drift,—seeming to slide with a swing from swell to swell,—ascending, sinking,—alternately presenting breast or shoulder to the wave; always diminishing more and more to the eyes of Mateo and Miguel,—till he becomes a moving speck, occasionally hard to follow through the confusion of heaping waters. . . . You are not afraid of the sharks, Feliu!—no: they are afraid of you; right and left they slunk away from your coming that morning you swam for life in West-Indian waters, with your knife in your teeth, while the balls of the Cuban coast-guard were purring all around you. That day the swarming sea was warm,—warm like soup—and clear, with an emerald flash in every ripple,—not opaque and clamorous like the Gulf to-day. . . . Miguel and his comrade are anxious. Ropes are unrolled and interknotted into a line. Miguel remains on the beach; but Mateo, bearing the end of the line, fights his way out,—swimming and wading by turns, to the farther sandbar, where the water is shallow enough to stand in,—if you know how to jump when the breaker comes.

But Feliu, nearing the flooded shell-bank, watches the white flashings,—knows when the time comes to keep flat and take a long, long breath. One heavy vol-

leying of foam,—darkness and hissing as of a steam-
burst; a vibrant lifting up; a rush into light,—and again
the volleying and the seething darkness. Once more,—
and the fight is won! He feels the upcoming chill of
deeper water,—sees before him the green quaking of
unbroken swells,—and far beyond him Mateo leaping
on the bar,—and beside him, almost within arm's
reach, a great billiard-table swaying, and a dead woman
clinging there, and . . . the child.

A moment more, and Feliu has lifted himself beside
the waifs. . . . How fast the dead woman clings, as if
with the one power which is strong as death,—the desperate force of love! Not in vain; for the frail creature
bound to the mother's corpse with a silken scarf has
still the strength to cry out:—"*Maman! maman!*" But
time is life now; and the tiny hands must be pulled
away from the fair dead neck, and the scarf taken to
bind the infant firmly to Feliu's broad shoulders,—
quickly, roughly; for the ebb will not wait. . . .

And now Feliu has a burden; but his style of swimming has totally changed;—he rises from the water
like a Triton, and his powerful arms seem to spin in
circles, like the spokes of a flying wheel. For now is the
wrestle indeed!—after each passing swell comes a
prodigious pulling from beneath,—the sea clutching
for its prey. But the reef is gained, is passed;—the wild
horses of the deep seem to know the swimmer who has
learned to ride them so well. And still the brown arms
spin in an ever-nearing mist of spray; and the outer
sand-bar is not far off,—and there is shouting Mateo,

leaping in the surf, swinging something about his head, as a vaquero swings his noose! . . . Sough! splash!—it struggles in the trough beside Feliu, and the sinewy hand descends upon it. *¡Tengo!—¡tira, Miguel!*[15] And their feet touch land again! . . .

She is very cold, the child, and very still, with eyes closed.

—"*¿Esta muerta, Feliu?*"[16] asks Mateo.

—"*¡No!*" the panting swimmer makes answer, emerging, while the waves reach whitely up the sand as in pursuit,—"*no; ¡vive! ¡respira todavía!*"[17]

Behind him the deep lifts up its million hands, and thunders as in acclaim.

IV.

—"*¡Madre de Dios!—¡mi sueño!*" screamed Carmen, abandoning her preparations for the morning meal, as Feliu, nude, like a marine god, rushed in and held out to her a dripping and gasping baby-girl,—"Mother of God! my dream!" But there was no time then to tell of dreams; the child might die. In one instant Carmen's quick, deft hands had stripped the slender little body; and while Mateo and Feliu were finding dry clothing and stimulants, and Miguel telling how it all happened—quickly, passionately, with furious gesture,— the kind and vigorous woman exerted all her skill to

---

15. "I have it!—pull, Miguel!"
16. "Is she dead?"
17. "No; she's alive! She's still breathing!"

revive the flickering life. Soon Feliu came to aid her, while his men set to work completing the interrupted preparation of the breakfast. Flannels were heated for the friction of the frail limbs; and brandy-and-water warmed, which Carmen administered by the spoonful, skilfully as any physician,—until, at last, the little creature opened her eyes and began to sob. Sobbing still, she was laid in Carmen's warm feather-bed, well swathed in woollen wrappings. The immediate danger, at least, was over; and Feliu smiled with pride and pleasure.

Then Carmen first ventured to relate her dream; and his face became grave again. Husband and wife gazed a moment into each other's eyes, feeling together the same strange thrill—that mysterious faint creeping, as of a wind passing, which is the awe of the Unknowable. Then they looked at the child, lying there, pink-cheeked with the flush of the blood returning; and such a sudden tenderness touched them as they had known long years before, while together bending above the slumbering loveliness of lost Conchita.

—"*¡Que ojos!*"[18] murmured Feliu, as he turned away,—feigning hunger. . . . (He was not hungry; but his sight had grown a little dim, as with a mist.) *¡Que ojos!* They were singular eyes, large, dark, and wonderfully fringed. The child's hair was yellow—it was the flash of it that had saved her; yet her eyes and brows were beautifully black. She was comely, but with such a curious, delicate comeliness—totally unlike the robust beauty of

18. "What eyes!"

Concha. . . . At intervals she would moan a little between her sobs; and at last cried out, with a thin, shrill cry: "*Maman!—oh! maman!*" Then Carmen lifted her from the bed to her lap, and caressed her, and rocked her gently to and fro, as she had done many a night for Concha,—murmuring,—"*¡Yo seré tu madre, angel mío, dulzura mía!—¡seré tu madrecita, palomita mía!*" (I will be thy mother, my angel, my sweet;—I will be thy little mother, my doveling.) And the long silk fringes of the child's eyes overlapped, shadowed her little cheeks; and she slept—just as Conchita had slept long ago,—with her head on Carmen's bosom.

Feliu re-appeared at the inner door: at a sign, he approached cautiously, without noise, and looked.

—"She can talk," whispered Carmen in Spanish: "she called her mother"—*ha llamado a su madre.*

—"*Y Dios también la ha llamado,*" responded Feliu, with rude pathos;—"*And God also called her.*"

—"But the Virgin sent us the child, Feliu,—sent us the child for Concha's sake."

He did not answer at once; he seemed to be thinking very deeply;—Carmen anxiously scanned his impassive face.

—"Who knows?" he answered, at last;—"who knows? Perhaps she has ceased to belong to any one else." . . .

One after another, Feliu's luggers fluttered in,—bearing with them news of the immense calamity. And all the fishermen, in turn, looked at the child. Not one had ever seen her before.

V.

Ten days later, a lugger full of armed men entered the bayou, and moored at Viosca's wharf. The visitors were, for the most part, country gentlemen,—residents of Franklin and neighboring towns, or planters from the Têche country,—forming one of the numerous expeditions organized for the purpose of finding the bodies of relatives or friends lost in the great hurricane, and of punishing the robbers of the dead. They had searched numberless nooks of the coast, had given sepulture to many corpses, had recovered a large amount of jewelry, and—as Feliu afterward learned,—had summarily tried and executed several of the most abandoned class of wreckers found with ill-gotten valuables in their possession, and convicted of having mutilated the drowned. But they came to Viosca's landing only to obtain information;—he was too well known and liked to be a subject for suspicion; and, moreover, he had one good friend in the crowd,—Captain Harris of New Orleans, a veteran steam-boat man and a market-contractor, to whom he had disposed of many a cargo of fresh *pómpano*, sheep's-head, and Spanish-mackerel. . . . Harris was the first to step to land;—some ten of the party followed him. Nearly all had lost some relative or friend in the great catastrophe;—the gathering was serious, silent,—almost grim,—which formed about Feliu.

Mateo, who had come to the country while a boy, spoke English better than the rest of the *chênière* people;—he acted as interpreter whenever Feliu found any difficulty in comprehending or answering questions; and he told them of the child rescued that wild morning, and of Feliu's swim. His recital evoked a murmur of interest and excitement, followed by a confusion of questions. Well, they could see for themselves, Feliu said; but he hoped they would have a little patience;— the child was still weak;—it might be dangerous to startle her. "We'll arrange it just as you like," responded the captain;—"go ahead, Feliu!" . . .

All proceeded to the house, under the great trees; Feliu and Captain Harris leading the way. It was sultry and bright;—even the sea-breeze was warm; there were pleasant odors in the shade, and a soporific murmur made of leaf-speech and the hum of gnats. Only the captain entered the house with Feliu; the rest remained without—some taking seats on a rude plank bench under the oaks—others flinging themselves down upon the weeds—a few stood still, leaning upon their rifles. Then Carmen came out to them with gourds and a bucket of fresh water, which all were glad to drink.

They waited many minutes. Perhaps it was the cool peace of the place that made them all feel how hot and tired they were: conversation flagged; and the general languor finally betrayed itself in a silence so absolute that every leaf-whisper seemed to become separately audible.

It was broken at last by the guttural voice of the old captain emerging from the cottage, leading the child by the hand, and followed by Carmen and Feliu. All who had been resting rose up and looked at the child.

Standing in a lighted space, with one tiny hand enveloped by the captain's great brown fist, she looked so lovely that a general exclamation of surprise went up. Her bright hair, loose and steeped in the sun-flame, illuminated her like a halo; and her large dark eyes, gentle and melancholy as a deer's, watched the strange faces before her with shy curiosity. She wore the same dress in which Feliu had found her—a soft white fabric of muslin, with trimmings of ribbon that had once been blue; and the now discolored silken scarf, which had twice done her such brave service, was thrown over her shoulders. Carmen had washed and repaired the dress very creditably; but the tiny slim feet were bare,—the brine-soaked shoes she wore that fearful night had fallen into shreds at the first attempt to remove them.

—"Gentlemen," said Captain Harris,—"we can find no clew to the identity of this child. There is no mark upon her clothing; and she wore nothing in the shape of jewelry—except this string of coral beads. We are nearly all Americans here; and she does not speak any English. . . . Does any one here know anything about her?"

Carmen felt a great sinking at her heart: was her new-found darling to be taken so soon from her? But no answer came to the captain's query. No one of the expedition had ever seen that child before. The coral beads were passed from hand to hand; the scarf was minutely scrutinized without avail. Somebody asked if the child could not talk German or Italian.

—"¿Italiano? ¡No!" said Feliu, shaking his head. . . . One of his luggermen, Gioachino Sparicio, who, though a Sicilian, could speak several Italian idioms besides his own, had already essayed.

—"She speaks something or other," answered the captain—"but no English. I couldn't make her understand me; and Feliu, who talks nearly all the infernal languages spoken down this way, says he can't make her understand him. Suppose some of you who know French talk to her a bit. . . . Laroussel, why don't you try?"

The young man addressed did not at first seem to notice the captain's suggestion. He was a tall, lithe fellow, with a dark, positive face: he had never removed his black gaze from the child since the moment of her appearance. Her eyes, too, seemed to be all for him—to return his scrutiny with a sort of vague pleasure, a half savage confidence. . . . Was it the first embryonic feeling of race-affinity quickening in the little brain?—some intuitive, inexplicable sense of kindred? She shrank from Doctor Hecker, who addressed her in German, shook her head at Lawyer Solari, who tried to make her answer in Italian; and her look always went back plaintively to the dark, sinister face of Laroussel,—Laroussel who had calmly taken a human life, a wicked human life, only the evening before.

—"Laroussel, you're the only Creole in this crowd," said the captain; "talk to her! Talk *gumbo*[19] to her! . . . I've no doubt this child knows German very well, and Italian too,"—he added, maliciously—"but not in the way you gentlemen pronounce it!"

Laroussel handed his rifle to a friend, crouched down before the little girl, and looked into her face, and smiled. Her great sweet orbs shone into his one moment, seriously, as if searching; and then . . . she

19. the term used by Americans in south Louisiana to refer to the Louisiana Creole dialect

returned his smile. It seemed to touch something latent within the man, something rare; for his whole expression changed; and there was a caress in his look and voice none of the men could have believed possible—as he exclaimed:—

—"*Fais moin bo, piti.*"[20]

She pouted up her pretty lips and kissed his black moustache.

He spoke to her again:—

—"*Dis moin to nom, piti;—dis moin to nom, chère.*"[21]

Then, for the first time, she spoke, answering in her argent treble:

—"*Zouzoune.*"

All held their breath. Captain Harris lifted his finger to his lips to command silence.

—"Zouzoune? Zouzoune qui, chère?"

—"Zouzoune, ça c'est moin, Lili!"

—"C'est pas tout to nom, Lili;—dis moin, chère, to laut nom."

—"Mo pas connin laut nom."

—"Comment yé té pélé to maman, piti?"

—"Maman,—Maman 'Dèle."

—"Et comment yé té pélé to papa, chère?"

—"Papa Zulien."

—"Bon! Et comment to maman té pélé to papa?—dis ça à moin, chère?"

The child looked down, put a finger in her mouth, thought a moment, and replied:—

—"Li pélé li, 'Chéri'; li pélé li, 'Papoute.'"

20. "Give me a kiss, little one."
21. "Tell me your name, little one;—tell me your name, dear."

—"Aïe, aïe!—c'est tout, ça?—to maman té jamain pélé li daut' chose?"

—"Mo pas connin, moin."

She began to play with some trinkets attached to his watch chain;—a very small gold compass especially impressed her fancy by the trembling and flashing of its tiny needle, and she murmured, coaxingly:—

—"Mo oulé ça! Donnin ça à moin."

He took all possible advantage of the situation, and replied at once:—

—"Oui! mo va donnin toi ça si to di moin to laut nom."

The splendid bribe evidently impressed her greatly; for tears rose to the brown eyes as she answered:

—"*Mo pas capab di' ça;—mo pas capab di' laut nom. . . .Mo oulé; mo pas capab!*"[22]

Laroussel explained. The child's name was Lili,—perhaps a contraction of Eulalie; and her pet Creole

---

22. —"Zouzoune what, dear?"

—"Zouzoune, that is I, Lili!"

—"That is not your whole name, Lili;—tell me, dear, your other name."

—"I don't know my other name."

—"What did you call your mamma, little one?"

—"Mamma,—Mama 'Dele."

—"And what did you call your papa, dear?

—"Papa Julien."

—"Good! And what did your mamma call your papa?—tell me that, dear?"
. . .
—"She calls him 'Dear;' she calls him 'Little Papa.'"

—"Sure, sure;—but did your mamma sometimes call him something else?"

—"I don't know."
. . .
—"I want this! Give it to me!"
. . .
—"O.K.! I'll give it to you if you tell me your other name."
. . .
"*I'm not able to tell you that,—I'm not able to tell you my other name. . . . I want it! I'm not able to!*"

name Zouzoune. He thought she must be the
daughter of wealthy people; but she could not, for
some reason or other, tell her family name. Perhaps
she could not pronounce it well, and was afraid of
being laughed at: some of the old French names were
very hard for Creole children to pronounce, so long
as the little ones were indulged in the habit of talking the patois; and after a certain age their mispro-
nunciations would be made fun of in order to accus-
tom them to abandon the idiom of the slave-nurses,
and to speak only French. Perhaps, again, she was
really unable to recall the name: certain memories
might have been blurred in the delicate brain by the
shock of that terrible night. She said her mother's
name was Adèle, and her father's Julien; but these
were very common names in Louisiana,—and could
afford scarcely any better clew than the innocent
statement that her mother used to address her father
as "dear" (*Chéri*),—or with the Creole diminutive
"little papa" (*Papoute*). Then Laroussel tried to reach
a clew in other ways, without success. He asked her
about where she lived,—what the place was like; and
she told him about fig-trees in a court, and galleries,[23]
and *banquettes*,[24] and spoke of a *faubou*,[25]—without
being able to name any street. He asked her what her
father used to do, and was assured that he did everything—that there was nothing he could not do.
Divine absurdity of childish faith!—infinite artless-
ness of childish love! . . . Probably the little girl's par-

---

23. wide and deep porch, typical Creole architecture
24. sidewalks
25. neighborhood

ents had been residents of New Orleans—dwellers of the old colonial quarter,—the faubourg, the *faubou'*.

—"Well, gentlemen," said Captain Harris, as Laroussel abandoned his cross-examination in despair,—"all we can do now is to make inquiries. I suppose we'd better leave the child here. She is very weak yet, and in no condition to be taken to the city, right in the middle of the hot season; and nobody could care for her any better than she's being cared for here. Then, again, seems to me that as Feliu saved her life,—and that at the risk of his own,—he's got the prior claim, anyhow; and his wife is just crazy about the child—wants to adopt her. If we can find her relatives so much the better; but I say, gentlemen, let them come right here to Feliu, themselves, and thank him as he ought to be thanked, by God! That's just what I think about it."

Carmen understood the little speech;—all the Spanish charm of her youth had faded out years before; but in the one swift look of gratitude she turned upon the captain, it seemed to blossom again;—for that quick moment, she was beautiful.

"The captain is quite right," observed Dr. Hecker: "it would be very dangerous to take the child away just now." There was no dissent.

—"All correct, boys?" asked the captain. . . . "Well, we've got to be going. By-by, Zouzoune!"

But Zouzoune burst into tears. Laroussel was going too!

—"Give her the thing, Laroussel! she gave you a kiss, anyhow—more than she'd do for me," cried the captain.

Laroussel turned, detached the little compass from his watch chain, and gave it to her. She held up her pretty face for his farewell kiss. . . .

VI.

But it seemed fated that Feliu's waif should never be identified;—diligent inquiry and printed announcements alike proved fruitless. Sea and sand had either hidden or effaced all the records of the little world they had engulfed: the annihilation of whole families, the extinction of races, had, in more than one instance, rendered vain all efforts to recognize the dead. It required the subtle perception of long intimacy to name remains tumefied and discolored by corruption and exposure, mangled and gnawed by fishes, by reptiles, and by birds;—it demanded the great courage of love to look upon the eyeless faces found sweltering in the blackness of cypress-shadows, under the low palmettoes of the swamps,—where gorged buzzards started from sleep, or cotton-mouths uncoiled, hissing, at the coming of the searchers. And sometimes all who had loved the lost were themselves among the missing. The full roll-call of names could never be made out; extraordinary mistakes were committed. Men whom the world deemed dead and buried came back, like ghosts,—to read their own epitaphs.

. . . Almost at the same hour that Laroussel was questioning the child in Creole patois, another expedition, searching for bodies along the coast, discovered on the beach of a low islet famed as a haunt of pelicans, the corpse of a child. Some locks of bright hair still adhering to the skull, a string of red beads, a white muslin dress, a handkerchief broidered with the initials "A. L. B.,"—were secured as clews; and the little body was interred where it had been found.

And, several days before, Captain Hotard, of the relief-boat *Estelle Brousseaux*, had found, drifting in the open Gulf (latitude 26° 43'; longitude 88° 17'),—the corpse of a fair-haired woman, clinging to a table. The body was disfigured beyond recognition: even the slender bones of the hands had been stripped by the nibs of the sea-birds—except one finger, the third of the left, which seemed to have been protected by a ring of gold, as by a charm. Graven within the plain yellow circlet was a date,—"JUILLET—1851"; and the names,—"ADÈLE + JULIEN,"—separated by a cross. The *Estelle* carried coffins that day: most of them were already full; but there was one for Adèle.

Who was she?—who was her Julien? . . . When the *Estelle* and many other vessels had discharged their ghastly cargoes;—when the bereaved of the land had assembled as hastily as they might for the duty of identification;—when memories were strained almost to madness in research of names, dates, incidents—for the evocation of dead words, resurrection of vanished days, recollection of dear promises,—then, in the confusion, it was believed and declared that the little corpse found on the pelican island was the daughter of the wearer of the wedding ring: Adèle La Brierre, *née* Florane, wife of Dr. Julien La Brierre, of New Orleans, who was numbered among the missing.

And they brought dead Adèle back,—up shadowy river windings, over linked brightnesses of lake and lakelet, through many a green glimmering bayou,—to the Creole city, and laid her to rest somewhere in the old Saint-Louis Cemetery. And upon the tablet recording her name were also graven the words—

. . . .
Aussi à la mémoire de
son mari;
JULIEN RAYMOND LA BRIERRE,
né à la paroisse St. Landry,
le 29 Mai; MDCCCXXVIII;
et de leur fille,
EULALIE,
agée de 4 ans et 5 mois,—
Qui tous périrent
dans la grande tempête qui
balayâ L'Île Dernière, le
10 Août, MDCCCLVI

. . . + . . .
Priez pour eux![26]

---

26. Also to the memory of
her husband;
Julien Raymond La Brierre
born in the parish of 29 May; 1833;
and of their daughter,
Eulalie,
age 4 years and 5 months,—
Who all perished
in the great storm which
swept Last Island, the
10 August, 1856
. . . + . . .
Pray for them!

VII.

Yet six months afterward the face of Julien La Brierre was seen again upon the streets of New Orleans. Men started at the sight of him, as at a spectre standing in the sun. And nevertheless the apparition cast a shadow. People paused, approached, half extended a hand through old habit, suddenly checked themselves and passed on,—wondering they should have forgotten, asking themselves why they had so nearly made an absurd mistake.

It was a February day,—one of those crystalline days of our snowless Southern winter, when the air is clear and cool, and outlines sharpen in the light as if viewed through the focus of a diamond glass;—and in that brightness Julien La Brierre perused his own brief epitaph, and gazed upon the sculptured name of drowned Adèle. Only half a year had passed since she was laid away in the high wall of tombs,—in that strange colonial columbarium where the dead slept in rows, behind squared marbles lettered in black or bronze. Yet her resting-place,—in the highest range,—already seemed old. Under our Southern sun, the vegetation of cemeteries seems to spring into being spontaneously—to leap all suddenly into luxuriant life! Microscopic mossy growths had begun to mottle the slab that closed her in;—over its face some singular creeper was crawling, planting tiny reptile-feet into the chiselled letters of the inscription; and from the moist soil below speckled euphorbias were growing up to her,—and morning

glories,—and beautiful green tangled things of which
he did not know the name.

And the sight of the pretty lizards, puffing their
crimson pouches in the sun, or undulating athwart epitaphs, and shifting their color when approached, from
emerald to ashen-gray;—the caravans of the ants, jour-
neying to and from tiny chinks in the masonry;—the
bees gathering honey from the crimson blossoms of the
crête-de-coq,[27] whose radicles sought sustenance, perhaps from human dust, in the decay of generations:—
all that rich life of graves summoned up fancies of Resurrection, Nature's resurrection-work—wondrous
transformations of flesh, marvellous transmigration of
souls! . . . From some forgotten crevice of that tomb
roof, which alone intervened between her and the vast
light, a sturdy weed was growing. He knew that plant,
as it quivered against the blue,—the *chou-gras*,[28] as Creole children call it: its dark berries form the mocking-
bird's favorite food. . . . Might not its roots, exploring
darkness, have found some unfamiliar nutriment
within?—might it not be that something of the dead
heart had risen to purple and emerald life—in the sap
of translucent leaves, in the wine of the savage
berries,—to blend with the blood of the Wizard
Singer,—to lend a strange sweetness to the melody of
his wooing? . . .

. . . Seldom, indeed, does it happen that a man in
the prime of youth, in the possession of wealth, habit-

27. cockscomb (*Celosia argentia*)—ornamental tropical plant native to Asia
28. coarse-cabbage; pokeweed (*Phytolacca americana*)—a plant whose leaves are
edible but whose roots are extremely toxic

uated to comforts and the elegances of life, discovers in one brief week how minute his true relation to the human aggregate,—how insignificant his part as one living atom of the social organism. Seldom, at the age of twenty-eight, has one been made able to comprehend, through experience alone, that in the vast and complex Stream of Being he counts for less than a drop; and that, even as the blood loses and replaces its corpuscles, without a variance in the volume and vigor of its current, so are individual existences eliminated and replaced in the pulsing of a people's life, with never a pause in its mighty murmur. But all this, and much more, Julien had learned in seven merciless days— seven successive and terrible shocks of experience. The enormous world had not missed him; and his place therein was not void—society had simply forgotten him. So long as he had moved among them, all he knew for friends had performed their petty altruistic *rôles*,—had discharged their small human obligations,—had kept turned toward him the least selfish side of their natures,—had made with him a tolerably equitable exchange of ideas and of favors; and after his disappearance from their midst, they had duly mourned for his loss—to themselves! They had played out the final act in the unimportant drama of his life: it was really asking too much to demand a repetition. . . . Impossible to deceive himself as to the feeling his unanticipated return had aroused:—feigned pity where he had looked for sympathetic welcome; dismay where he had expected surprised delight; and, oftener, airs of resignation, or disappointment ill disguised,—always insincerity, politely masked or coldly bare. He had come back to find strangers in his home, relatives at law concerning his estate, and himself regarded as an intruder among the living,—an unlucky guest, a *revenant*[29]. . . . How hollow and selfish a world it seemed! And yet there was love in it; he had been loved in it, unselfishly, passionately, with the love of father and of mother, of wife and child. . . . All buried!—all lost forever! . . . Oh! would to God the story of that stone were not a lie!— would to kind God he also were dead! . . .

Evening shadowed: the violet deepened and prickled itself with stars;—the sun passed below the west, leaving in his wake a momentary splendor of vermilion . . . our Southern day is not prolonged by gloaming. And Julien's thoughts darkened with the darkening, and as swiftly. For while there was yet light to see, he read another name that he used to know—the name of RAMÍREZ . . . *Nació en Cienfuegos, isla de Cuba*[30]. . . . Wherefore born?—for what eternal purpose, Ramírez,—in the City of a Hundred Fires? He had blown out his brains before the sepulchre of his young wife. . . . It was a detached double vault, shaped like a huge chest, and much dilapidated already:—under the continuous burrowing of the crawfish it had sunk greatly on one side, tilting as if about to fall. Out from its zigzag fissurings of brick and plaster, a sinister voice seemed to come:—"*Go thou and do likewise! . . . Earth groans with her burthen even now,—the burthen of Man: she holds no place for thee!*"

---

29. ghost
30. Born in Cienfuegos ["Hundred Fires"], island of Cuba.

VIII.

. . . That voice pursued him into the darkness of his chilly room,—haunted him in the silence of his lodging. And then began within the man that ghostly struggle between courage and despair, between patient reason and mad revolt, between weakness and force, between darkness and light, which all sensitive and generous natures must wage in their own souls at least once—perhaps many times—in their lives. Memory, in such moments, plays like an electric storm;—all involuntarily he found himself reviewing his life.

Incidents long forgotten came back with singular vividness: he saw the Past as he had not seen it while it was the Present;—remembrances of home, recollections of infancy, recurred to him with terrible intensity,—the artless pleasures and the trifling griefs, the little hurts and the tender pettings, the hopes and the anxieties of those who loved him, the smiles and tears of slaves. . . . And his first Creole pony, a present from his father the day after he had proved himself able to recite his prayers correctly in French, without one mispronunciation—without saying *crasse* for *grâce*;—and yellow Michel, who taught him to swim and to fish and to paddle a pirogue;[31]—and the bayou, with its wonder-world of turtles and birds and creeping things;—and his German tutor, who could not pronounce the *j*;—and the songs of the cane-fields,—strangely pleasing, full of

---

31. small, flat-bottomed boat used in shallow waters of south Louisiana

quaverings and long plaintive notes, like the call of the cranes. . . . *Tou', tou' pays blanc!* . . . Afterward Camanière had leased the place;—everything must have been changed; even the songs could not be the same. *Tou', tou' pays blanc!—Danié qui commandé.* . . .

And then Paris; and the university, with its wild under-life,—some debts, some follies; and the frequent fond letters from home to which he might have replied so much oftener;—Paris, where talent is mediocrity; Paris, with its thunders and its splendors and its seething of passion;—Paris, supreme focus of human endeavor, with its madnesses of art, its frenzied striving to express the Inexpressible, its spasmodic strainings to clutch the Unattainable, its soarings of soul-fire to the heaven of the Impossible. . . .

What a rejoicing there was at his return!—how radiant and level the long Road of the Future seemed to open before him!—everywhere friends, prospects, felicitations. Then his first serious love;—and the night of the ball at St. Martinsville,—the vision of light! Gracile as a palm, and robed at once so simply, so exquisitely in white, she had seemed to him the supreme realization of all possible dreams of beauty. . . . And his passionate jealousy; and the slap from Laroussel; and the humiliating two-minute duel with rapiers in which he learned that he had found his master. The scar was deep. Why had not Laroussel killed him then? . . . Not evil-hearted, Laroussel,—they used to salute each other afterward when they met; and Laroussel's smile was kindly. Why had he refrained from returning it? Where was Laroussel now?

For the death of his generous father, who had sacrificed so much to reform him; for the death, only a short while after, of his all-forgiving mother, he had found one sweet woman to console him with her tender words, her loving lips, her delicious caress. She had given him Zouzoune, the darling link between their lives,—Zouzoune, who waited each evening with black Églantine at the gate to watch for his coming, and to cry through all the house like a bird, "*Papa, lapé vini!—papa Zulien apé vini!*" . . . And once that she had made him very angry by upsetting the ink over a mass of business papers, and he had slapped her (could he ever forgive himself?)—she had cried, through her sobs of astonishment and pain:—"*To laimin moin?—to batté moin!*" (Thou lovest me?—thou beatest me!) Next month she would have been five years old. To laimin moin?—to batté moin! . . .

A furious paroxysm of grief convulsed him, suffocated him; it seemed to him that something within must burst, must break. He flung himself down upon his bed, biting the coverings in order to stifle his outcry, to smother the sounds of his despair. What crime had he ever done, oh God! that he should be made to suffer thus?—was it for this he had been permitted to live? had been rescued from the sea and carried round all the world unscathed? Why should he live to remember, to suffer, to agonize? Was not Ramírez wiser?

How long the contest within him lasted, he never knew; but ere it was done, he had become, in more ways than one, a changed man. For the first,—though not indeed for the last time,—something of the deeper and nobler comprehension of human weakness and of human suffering had been revealed to him,—something of that larger knowledge without which the sense of duty can never be fully acquired, nor the understanding of unselfish goodness, nor the spirit of tenderness. The suicide is not a coward; he is an egotist.

A ray of sunlight touched his wet pillow,—awoke him. He rushed to the window, flung the latticed shutters apart, and looked out.

Something beautiful and ghostly filled all the vistas,—frost-haze; and in some queer way the mist had momentarily caught and held the very color of the sky. An azure fog! Through it the quaint and checkered street—as yet but half illumined by the sun,—took tones of impossible color; the view paled away through faint bluish tints into transparent purples;—all the shadows were indigo. How sweet the morning!—how well life seemed worth living! Because the sun had shown his face through a fairy veil of frost! . . .

Who was the ancient thinker?—was it Hermes?—who said:—

"*The Sun is Laughter; for 'tis He who maketh joyous the thoughts of men, and gladdeneth the infinite world.*" . . .

Part III

THE SHADOW OF THE TIDE

I.

Carmen found that her little pet had been taught how to pray; for each night and morning when the devout woman began to make her orisons, the child would kneel beside her, with little hands joined, and in a voice sweet and clear murmur something she had learned by heart. Much as this pleased Carmen, it seemed to her that the child's prayers could not be wholly valid unless uttered in Spanish;—for Spanish was heaven's own tongue,—*la lengua de Dios, el idioma de Dios*; and she resolved to teach her to say the *Salve María* and the *Padre Nuestro*[32] in Castilian,—also, her own favorite

---

32. the *Hail Mary* and the *Our Father*

prayer to the Virgin, beginning with the words, "*Madre santísima, toda dulce y hermosa.*" . . .[33]

So Conchita—for a new name had been given to her with that terrible sea christening—received her first lessons in Spanish; and she proved a most intelligent pupil. Before long she could prattle to Feliu;—she would watch for his return of evenings, and announce his coming with "*¡Aquí viene mi papacito!*"—she learned, too, from Carmen, many little caresses of speech to greet him with. Feliu's was not a joyous nature; he had his dark hours, his sombre days; yet it was rarely that he felt too sullen to yield to the little one's petting, when she would leap up to reach his neck and to coax his kiss, with—"*¡Dame un beso, papa!—así;—¡y otro! ¡otro! ¡otro!**" He grew to love her like his own;—was she not indeed his own, since he had won her from death? And none had yet come to dispute his claim. More and more, with the passing of weeks, months, seasons, she became a portion of his life—a part of all that he wrought for. At the first, he had had a half-formed hope that the little one might be reclaimed by relatives generous and rich enough to insist upon his acceptance of a handsome compensation; and that Carmen could find some solace in a pleasant visit to Barceloneta. But now he felt that no possible generosity could requite him for her loss; and with the unconscious selfishness of affection, he commenced to dread her identification as a great calamity.

---

33. most saintly Mother, all sweet and beautiful

It was evident that she had been brought up nicely. She had pretty prim ways of drinking and eating, queer little fashions of sitting in company, and of addressing people. She had peculiar notions about colors in dress, about wearing her hair; and she seemed to have already imbibed a small stock of social prejudices not altogether in harmony with the republicanism of Viosca's Point. Occasional swarthy visitors,—men of the Manilla settlements,—she spoke of contemptuously as *nègues-marrons*;[34] and once she shocked Carmen inexpressibly by stopping in the middle of her evening prayer, declaring that she wanted to say her prayers to a *white* Virgin; Carmen's Señora de Guadalupe[35] was only a *negra!*[36] Then, for the first time, Carmen spoke so crossly to the child as to frighten her. But the pious woman's heart smote her the next moment for that first harsh word;—and she caressed the motherless one, consoled her, cheered her, and at last explained to her—I know not how—something very wonderful about the little figurine, something that made Chita's eyes big with awe. Thereafter she always regarded the Virgin of Wax as an object mysterious and holy.

And, one by one, most of Chita's little eccentricities were gradually eliminated from her developing life and thought. More rapidly than ordinary children, because singularly intelligent, she learned to adapt herself to all the changes of her new environment,—retaining only that indescribable something which to an experienced eye tells of hereditary refinement of habit and of

34. escaped blacks; slaves
35. the Virgin icon of Latin America
36. Spanish, feminine form, for black; here a black female person, or negresse

mind:—a natural grace, a thorough-bred ease and elegance of movement, a quickness and delicacy of perception.

She became strong again and active—active enough
to play a great deal on the beach, when the sun was not
too fierce; and Carmen made a canvas bonnet to shield
her head and face. Never had she been allowed to play
so much in the sun before; and it seemed to do her
good, though her little bare feet and hands became
brown as copper. At first, it must be confessed, she
worried her foster-mother a great deal by various queer
misfortunes and extraordinary freaks;—getting bitten
by crabs, falling into the bayou while in pursuit of
"fiddlers," or losing herself at the conclusion of desperate efforts to run races at night with the moon, or to
walk to the "end of the world." If she could only once
get to the edge of the sky, she said, she "could climb
up." She wanted to see the stars, which were the souls
of good little children; and she knew that God would
let her climb up. "Just what I am afraid of!"—thought
Carmen to herself;—"He might let her climb up,—a
little ghost!" But one day naughty Chita received a terrible lesson,—a lasting lesson,—which taught her the
value of obedience.

She had been particularly cautioned not to venture
into a certain part of the swamp in the rear of the
grove, where the weeds were very tall; for Carmen was
afraid some snake might bite the child. But Chita's
bird-bright eye had discerned a gleam of white in that
direction; and she wanted to know what it was. The
white could only be seen from one point, behind the
farthest house, where the ground was high. "Never go

there," said Carmen; "there is a Dead Man there,—will bite you!" And yet, one day, while Carmen was unusually busy, Chita went there.

In the early days of the settlement, a Spanish fisherman had died; and his comrades had built him a little tomb with the surplus of the same bricks and other material brought down the bayou for the construction of Viosca's cottages. But no one, except perhaps some wandering duck hunter, had approached the sepulchre for years. High weeds and grasses wrestled together all about it, and rendered it totally invisible from the surrounding level of the marsh.

Fiddlers swarmed away as Chita advanced over the moist soil, each uplifting its single huge claw as it sidled off;—then frogs began to leap before her as she reached the thicker grass;—and long-legged brown insects sprang showering to right and left as she parted the tufts of the thickening verdure. As she went on, the bitter-weeds disappeared;—jointed grasses and sinewy dark plants of a taller growth rose above her head: she was almost deafened by the storm of insect shrilling, and the mosquitoes became very wicked. All at once something long and black and heavy wriggled almost from under her naked feet,—squirming so horribly that for a minute or two she could not move for fright. But it slunk away somewhere, and hid itself; the weeds it had shaken ceased to tremble in its wake; and her courage returned. She felt such an exquisite and fearful pleasure in the gratification of that naughty curiosity! Then, quite unexpectedly—oh! what a start it gave her!—the solitary white object

burst upon her view, leprous and ghastly as the yawn
of a cotton-mouth. Tombs ruin soon in Louisiana;—
the one Chita looked upon seemed ready to topple
down. There was a great ragged hole at one end, where
wind and rain, and perhaps also the burrowing of
crawfish and of worms, had loosened the bricks, and
caused them to slide out of place. It seemed very black
inside; but Chita wanted to know what was there. She
pushed her way through a gap in the thin and rotten
line of pickets, and through some tall weeds with big
coarse pink flowers;—then she crouched down on
hands and knees before the black hole, and peered in.
It was not so black inside as she had thought; for a
sunbeam slanted down through a chink in the roof;
and she could see!

A brown head—without hair, without eyes, but
with teeth, ever so many teeth!—seemed to laugh at
her; and close to it sat a Toad, the hugest she had ever
seen; and the white skin of his throat kept puffing out
and going in. And Chita screamed and screamed, and
fled in wild terror,—screaming all the way, till Carmen
ran out to meet her and carry her home. Even when
safe in her adopted mother's arms, she sobbed with
fright. To the vivid fancy of the child there seemed to
be some hideous relation between the staring reptile
and the brown death's-head, with its empty eyes, and
its nightmare-smile.

The shock brought on a fever,—a fever that lasted
several days, and left her very weak. But the experience
taught her to obey, taught her that Carmen knew best
what was for her good. It also caused her to think a

great deal. Carmen had told her that the dead people never frightened good little girls who stayed at home.

—"Madrecita[37] Carmen," she asked, "is my mamma dead?"

—"*¡Pobrecita!* . . . Yes, my angel. God called her to Him,—your darling mother."

—"Madrecita," she asked again,—her young eyes growing vast with horror,—"is my own mamma now like *That?*" . . . She pointed toward the place of the white gleam, behind the great trees.

—"No, no, no! my darling!" cried Carmen, appalled herself by the ghastly question,—"your mamma is with the dear, good, loving God, who lives in the beautiful sky, above the clouds, my darling, beyond the sun!"

But Carmen's kind eyes were full of tears; and the child read their meaning. He who teareth off the Mask of the Flesh had looked into her face one unutterable moment:—she had seen the brutal Truth, naked to the bone!

Yet there came to her a little thrill of consolation, caused by the words of the tender falsehood; for that which she had discerned by day could not explain to her that which she saw almost nightly in her slumber. The face, the voice, the form of her loving mother still lived somewhere,—could not have utterly passed away; since the sweet presence came to her in dreams, bending and smiling over her, caressing her, speaking to her,—sometimes gently chiding, but always chiding with a kiss. And then the child would laugh in her sleep,

37. "little mother"

and prattle in Creole,—talking to the luminous shadow, telling the dead mother all the little deeds and thoughts of the day. . . . Why would God only let her come at night?

. . . Her idea of God had been first defined by the sight of a quaint French picture of the Creation,—an engraving which represented a shoreless sea under a black sky, and out of the blackness a solemn and bearded gray head emerging, and a cloudy hand through which stars glimmered. God was like old Doctor de Coulanges, who used to visit the house, and talk in a voice like a low roll of thunder. . . . At a later day, when Chita had been told that God was "everywhere at the same time"—without and within, beneath and above all things,—this idea became somewhat changed. The awful bearded face, the huge shadowy hand, did not fade from her thought; but they became fantastically blended with the larger and vaguer notion of something that filled the world and reached to the stars,—something diaphanous and incomprehensible like the invisible air, omnipresent and everlasting like the high blue of heaven. . . .

II.

. . . She began to learn the life of the coast.

With her acquisition of another tongue, there came to her also the understanding of many things relating to the world of the sea. She memorized with novel delight much that was told her day by day con-

cerning the nature surrounding her,—many secrets of
the air, many of those signs of heaven which the
dwellers in cities cannot comprehend because the
atmosphere is thickened and made stagnant above
them—cannot even watch because the horizon is
hidden from their eyes by walls, and by weary
avenues of trees with whitewashed trunks. She
learned, by listening, by asking, by observing also,
how to know the signs that foretell wild weather:—
tremendous sunsets, scuddings and bridgings of
cloud,—sharpening and darkening of the sea-line,—
and the shriek of gulls flashing to land in level flight,
out of a still transparent sky,—and halos about the
moon.

She learned where the sea-birds, with white bosoms
and brown wings, made their hidden nests of sand,—
and where the cranes waded for their prey,—and where
the beautiful wild-ducks, plumaged in satiny lilac and
silken green, found their food,—and where the best
reeds grew to furnish stems for Feliu's red-clay pipe,—
and where the ruddy sea-beans were most often tossed
upon the shore,—and how the gray pelicans fished all
together, like men—moving in far-extending semicir-
cles, beating the flood with their wings to drive the fish
before them.

And from Carmen she learned the fables and the
sayings of the sea,—the proverbs about its deafness, its
avarice, its treachery, its terrific power,—especially one
that haunted her for all time thereafter: *Si quieres
aprender a orar, entra en el mar* (If thou wouldst learn
to pray, go to the sea). She learned why the sea is salt,—
how "the tears of women made the waves of the sea,"—

and how the sea has "no friends,"—and how the cat's eyes change with the tides.

What had she lost of life by her swift translation from the dusty existence of cities to the open immensity of nature's freedom? What did she gain?

Doubtless she was saved from many of those little bitternesses and restraints and disappointments which all well-bred city children must suffer in the course of their training for the more or less factitious life of society:—obligations to remain very still with every nimble nerve quivering in dumb revolt;—the injustice of being found troublesome and being sent to bed early for the comfort of her elders;—the cruel necessity of straining her pretty eyes, for many long hours at a time, over grimy desks in gloomy school-rooms, though birds might twitter and bright winds flutter in the trees without;—the austere constraint and heavy drowsiness of warm churches, filled with the droning echoes of a voice preaching incomprehensible things;—the progressively augmenting weariness of lessons in deportment, in dancing, in music, in the impossible art of keeping her dresses unruffled and unsoiled. Perhaps she never had any reason to regret all these.

She went to sleep and awakened with the wild birds;—her life remained as unfettered by formalities as her fine feet by shoes. Excepting Carmen's old prayer-book,—in which she learned to read a little,—her childhood passed without books,—also without pictures, without dainties, without music, without theatrical amusements. But she saw and heard and felt much of that which, though old as the heavens and the earth, is yet eternally new and eternally young with the holiness of beauty,—eternally mystical and divine,—eternally weird: the unveiled magnificence of Nature's moods,—the perpetual poem hymned by wind and surge,—the everlasting splendor of the sky.

She saw the quivering pinkness of waters curled by the breath of the morning—under the deepening of the dawn—like a far fluttering and scattering of rose-leaves of fire;—

Saw the shoreless, cloudless, marvellous double-circling azure of perfect summer days—twin glories of infinite deeps inter-reflected, while the Soul of the World lay still, suffused with a jewel-light, as of vaporized sapphire;—

Saw the Sea shift color,—"change sheets,"—when the viewless Wizard of the Wind breathed upon its face, and made it green;—

Saw the immeasurable panics,—noiseless, scintillant,—which silver, summer after summer, curved leagues of beach with bodies of little fish—the yearly massacre of migrating populations, nations of sea-trout, driven from their element by terror;—and the winnowing of shark-fins,—and the rushing of porpoises,—and the rising of the *grande-écaille*, like a pillar of flame,—and the diving and pitching and fighting of the frigates and the gulls,—and the armored hordes of crabs swarming out to clear the slope after the carnage and the gorging had been done;—

Saw the Dreams of the Sky,—scudding mockeries of ridged foam,—and shadowy stratification of capes and coasts and promontories long-drawn-out,—and imageries, multicolored, of mountain frondage, and sierras whitening above sierras,—and phantom islands ringed around with lagoons of glory;—

Saw the toppling and smouldering of cloud-worlds after the enormous conflagration of sunsets,—incandescence ruining into darkness; and after it a moving and climbing of stars among the blacknesses,—like searching lamps;—

Saw the deep kindle countless ghostly candles as for mysterious night-festival,—and a luminous billowing under a black sky, and effervescences of fire, and the twirling and crawling of phosphoric foam;—

Saw the mesmerism of the Moon;—saw the enchanted tides self-heaped in muttering obeisance before her.

Often she heard the Music of the Marsh through the night: an infinity of flutings and tinklings made by tiny amphibia,—like the low blowing of numberless little tin horns, the clanking of billions of little bells;—and, at intervals, profound tones, vibrant and heavy, as of a bass viol—the orchestra of the great frogs! And interweaving with it all, one continuous shrilling,—keen as the steel speech of a saw,—the stridulous telegraphy of crickets.

But always,—always, dreaming or awake, she heard the huge blind Sea chanting that mystic and eternal hymn, which none may hear without awe, which no musician can learn;—

Heard the hoary Preacher,—*El Pregonador*,— preaching the ancient Word, the word "as a fire, and as a hammer that breaketh the rock in pieces,"—the Elohim-Word of the Sea! . . .

Unknowingly she came to know the immemorial sympathy of the mind with the Soul of the World,— the melancholy wrought by its moods of gray, the reverie responsive to its vagaries of mist, the exhilaration of its vast exultings—days of windy joy, hours of transfigured light.

She felt,—even without knowing it,—the weight of the Silences, the solemnities of sky and sea in these low regions where all things seem to dream—waters and grasses with their momentary wavings,—woods gray-webbed with mosses that drip and drool,—horizons with their delusions of vapor,—cranes meditating in their marshes,—kites floating in the high blue. . . . Even the children were singularly quiet; and their play less noisy—though she could not have learned the difference—than the play of city children. Hour after hour, the women sewed or wove in silence. And the brown men,—always barefooted, always wearing rough blue shirts,—seemed, when they lounged about the wharf on idle days, as if they had told each other long ago all they knew or could ever know, and had nothing more to say. They would stare at the flickering of the current, at the drifting of clouds and buzzards— seldom looking at each other, and always turning their black eyes again, in a weary way, to sky or sea. Even thus one sees the horses and the cattle of the coast, seeking the beach to escape the whizzing flies;—all watch the long waves rolling in, and sometimes turn their heads a moment to look at one another, but always look back to the waves again, as if wondering at a mystery. . . .

How often she herself had wondered—wondered at the multiform changes of each swell as it came in—transformations of tint, of shape, of motion, that seemed to betoken a life infinitely more subtle than the strange cold life of lizards and of fishes,—and sinister, and spectral. Then they all appeared to move in order,—according to one law or impulse;—each had its own voice, yet all sang one and the same everlasting song. Vaguely, as she watched them and listened to them, there came to her the idea of a unity of *will* in their motion, a unity of *menace* in their utterance—the idea of one monstrous and complex life! The sea *lived*: it could crawl backward and forward; it could speak!—it only feigned deafness and sightlessness for some malevolent end. Thenceforward she feared to find herself alone with it. Was it not at her that it strove to rush, muttering, and showing its white teeth, . . . just because it knew that she was all by herself? . . . *Si quieres aprender a orar, entra en el mar!* And Concha had well learned to pray. But the sea seemed to her the one Power which God could not make to obey Him as He pleased. Saying the creed one day, she repeated very slowly the opening words,—"*Creo en un Dios, padre todopoderoso, Criador de cielo y de la tierra,*"[38]—and paused and thought. *Creator of Heaven and Earth?* "Madrecita Carmen," she asked,— "*¿quién entonces hizó el mar?*" (who then made the sea?).

—"Dios, mi querida," answered Carmen.—"God, my darling. . . . All things were made by Him" (*todas las cosas fueron hechas por Él*).

---

38. the Catholic *Credo*, or *Confession of Faith*: "I believe in God, the Father Almighty, Creator of heaven and earth. . . ."

Even the wicked Sea! And He had said unto it: "Thus far, and no farther." . . . Was that why it had not overtaken and devoured her when she ran back in fear from the sudden reaching out of its waves? *Thus far . . . ?* But there were times when it disobeyed—when it rushed farther, shaking the world! Was it because God was then asleep—could not hear, did not see, until too late?

And the tumultuous ocean terrified her more and more: it filled her sleep with enormous nightmare;—it came upon her in dreams, mountain-shadowing,— holding her with its spell, smothering her power of outcry, heaping itself to the stars.

Carmen became alarmed;—she feared that the nervous and delicate child might die in one of those moaning dreams out of which she had to arouse her, night after night. But Feliu, answering her anxiety with one of his favorite proverbs, suggested a heroic remedy:—

—"The world is like the sea: those who do not know how to swim in it are drowned;—and the sea is like the world," he added. . . . "Chita must learn to swim!"

And he found the time to teach her. Each morning, at sunrise, he took her into the water. She was less terrified the first time than Carmen thought she would be;—she seemed to feel confidence in Feliu; although she screamed piteously before her first ducking at his hands. His teaching was not gentle. He would carry her out, perched upon his shoulder, until the water rose to his own neck; and there he would throw her from him, and let her struggle to reach him again as best she could. The first few mornings she had to be pulled out almost at once; but after that Feliu showed her less mercy, and helped her only when he saw she was really in danger. He attempted no other instruction until she had learned that in order to save herself from being half choked by the salt water, she must not scream; and by the time she became habituated to these austere experiences, she had already learned by instinct alone how to keep herself afloat for awhile, how to paddle a little with her hands. Then he commenced to train her to use them,—to lift them well out and throw them forward as if reaching, to dip them as the blade of an oar is dipped at an angle, without loud splashing;—and he showed her also how to use her feet. She learned rapidly and astonishingly well. In less than two months Feliu felt really proud at the progress made by his tiny pupil: it was a delight to watch her lifting her slender arms above the water in swift, easy curves, with the same fine grace that marked all her other natural motions. Later on he taught her not to fear the sea even when it growled a little,—how to ride a swell, how to face a breaker, how to dive. She only needed practice thereafter; and Carmen, who could also swim, finding the child's health improving marvellously under this new discipline, took good care that Chita should practice whenever the mornings were not too cold, or the water too rough.

With the first thrill of delight at finding herself able to glide over the water unassisted, the child's superstitious terror of the sea passed away. Even for the adult there are few physical joys keener than the exultation of the swimmer;—how much greater the same glee as newly felt by an imaginative child,—a child, whose vivid fancy can lend unutterable value to the most insignificant trifles, can transform a weed-patch to an Eden! . . . Of her own accord she would ask for her morning bath, as soon as she opened her eyes;—it even required some severity to prevent her from remaining in the water too long. The sea appeared to her as something that had become tame for her sake, something that loved her in a huge rough way; a tremendous playmate, whom she no longer feared to see come bounding and barking to lick her feet. And, little by little, she also learned the wonderful healing and caressing power of the monster, whose cool embrace at once dispelled all drowsiness, feverishness, weariness,—even after the sultriest nights when the air had seemed to burn, and the mosquitoes had filled the chamber with a sound as of water boiling in many kettles. And on mornings when the sea was in too wicked a humor to be played with, how she felt the loss of her loved sport, and prayed for calm! Her delicate constitution changed;—the soft, pale flesh became firm and brown, the meagre limbs rounded into robust symmetry, the thin cheeks grew peachy with richer life; for the strength of the sea had entered into her; the sharp breath of the sea had renewed and brightened her young blood. . . .

. . . Thou primordial Sea, the awfulness of whose antiquity hath stricken all mythology dumb;—thou most wrinkled living Sea, the millions of whose years outnumber even the multitude of thy hoary motions;—thou omniform and most mysterious Sea, mother of the monsters and the gods,—whence thine eternal youth? Still do thy waters hold the infinite thrill of that Spirit which brooded above their face in the Beginning!—still is thy quickening breath an elixir unto them that flee to thee for life,—like the breath of young girls, like the breath of children, prescribed for the senescent by magicians of old,—prescribed unto weazened elders in the books of the Wizards.

III.

. . . Eighteen hundred and sixty-seven;—midsummer in the pest-smitten city of New Orleans.

Heat motionless and ponderous. The steel-blue of the sky bleached from the furnace-circle of the horizon;—the lukewarm river ran yellow and noiseless as a torrent of fluid wax. Even sounds seemed blunted by the heaviness of the air;—the rumbling of wheels, the reverberation of footsteps, fell half-toned upon the ear, like sounds that visit a dozing brain.

Daily, almost at the same hour, the continuous sense of atmospheric oppression became thickened;—a packed herd of low-bellying clouds lumbered up from the Gulf; crowded blackly against the sun; flickered, thundered, and burst in torrential rain—tepid, perpendicular—and vanished utterly away. Then, more furiously than before, the sun flamed down;—roofs and pavements steamed; the streets seemed to smoke; the air grew suffocating with vapor; and the luminous city filled with a faint, sickly odor,—a stale smell, as of dead leaves suddenly disinterred from wet mould,—as of grasses decomposing after a flood. Something saffron speckled the slimy water of the gutters; sulphur some called it; others feared even to give it a name! Was it only the wind-blown pollen of some innocuous plant? I do not know; but to many it seemed as if the Invisible Destruction were scattering visible seed! . . . Such were the days; and each day the terror-stricken city offered up its hecatomb to death; and the faces of all the dead were yellow as flame!

"DÉCÉDÉ—"; "DÉCÉDÉE—"; "FALLECIÓ";— "DIED." . . . On the door-posts, the telegraph-poles, the pillars of verandas, the lamps,—over the government letter-boxes,—everywhere glimmered the white annunciations of death. All the city was spotted with them. And lime was poured into the gutters; and huge purifying fires were kindled after sunset.

The nights began with a black heat;—there were hours when the acrid air seemed to ferment for stagnation, and to burn the bronchial tubing;—then, toward morning, it would grow chill with venomous vapors, with morbific dews,—till the sun came up to lift the torpid moisture, and to fill the buildings with ovenglow. And the interminable procession of mourners and hearses and carriages again began to circulate between the centres of life and of death;—and long trains and steam-ships rushed from the port, with heavy burden of fugitives.

Wealth might flee; yet even in flight there was peril. Men, who might have been saved by the craft of experienced nurses at home, hurriedly departed in apparent health, unconsciously carrying in their blood the toxic principle of a malady unfamiliar to physicians of the West and North;—and they died upon their way, by the road-side, by the river-banks, in woods, in deserted stations, on the cots of quarantine hospitals. Wiser those who sought refuge in the purity of the pine forests, or in those near Gulf Islands, whence the bright sea-breath kept ever sweeping back the expanding poison into the funereal swamps, into the misty lowlands. The watering-resorts became over-crowded;—then the fishing villages were thronged,—at least all which were easy to reach by steam-boat or by lugger. And at last, even Viosca's Point,—remote and unfamiliar as it was,—had a stranger to shelter: a good old gentleman named Edwards, rather broken down in health—who came as much for quiet as for sea-air, and who had been warmly recommended to Feliu by Captain Harris. For some years he had been troubled by a disease of the heart.

Certainly the old invalid could not have found a more suitable place so far as rest and quiet were concerned. The season had early given such little promise that several men of the Point betook themselves elsewhere; and the aged visitor had two or three vacant cabins from among which to select a dwelling-place. He chose to occupy the most remote of all, which Carmen furnished for him with a cool moss bed and some necessary furniture,—including a big wooden rocking-chair. It seemed to him very comfortable thus. He took his meals with the family, spent most of the day in his own quarters, spoke very little, and lived so unobtrusively and inconspicuously that his presence in the settlement was felt scarcely more than that of some dumb creature,—some domestic animal,—some humble pet whose relation to the family is only fully comprehended after it has failed to appear for several days in its accustomed place of patient waiting,—and we know that it is dead.

IV.

Persistently and furiously, at half-past two o'clock of an August morning, Sparicio rang Dr. La Brierre's nightbell. He had fifty dollars in his pocket, and a letter to deliver. He was to earn another fifty dollars—deposited in Feliu's hands,—by bringing the Doctor to Viosca's Point. He had risked his life for that money,—and was terribly in earnest.

Julien descended in his under-clothing, and opened the letter by the light of the hall lamp. It enclosed a check for a larger fee than he had ever before received, and contained an urgent request that he would at once accompany Sparicio to Viosca's Point,—as the sender was in hourly danger of death. The letter, penned in a long, quavering hand, was signed,—"*Henry Edwards.*"

His father's dear old friend! Julien could not refuse to go,—though he feared it was a hopeless case. *Angina pectoris*,—and a third attack at seventy years of age! Would it even be possible to reach the sufferer's bedside in time? "*Duè giorno,—con vento,*"[39]—said Sparicio.

Still, he must go; and at once. It was Friday morning;—might reach the Point Saturday night, with a
good wind. . . . He roused his housekeeper, gave all
needful instructions, prepared his little medicine-
chest;—and long before the first rose-gold fire of day
had flashed to the city spires, he was sleeping the sleep
of exhaustion in the tiny cabin of a fishing-sloop.

. . . For eleven years Julien had devoted himself,
heart and soul, to the exercise of that profession he had
first studied rather as a polite accomplishment than as
a future calling. In the unselfish pursuit of duty he had
found the only possible consolation for his irreparable
loss; and when the war came to sweep away his wealth,
he entered the struggle valorously, not to strive against
men, but to use his science against death. After the
passing of that huge shock, which left all the imposing
and splendid fabric of Southern feudalism wrecked
forever, his profession stood him in good stead;—he
found himself not only able to supply those personal
wants he cared to satisfy, but also to alleviate the misery of many whom he had known in days of opu-
lence;—the princely misery that never doffed its smiling mask, though living in secret, from week to week,
on bread and orange-leaf tea;—the misery that affected
condescension in accepting an invitation to dine,—
staring at the face of a watch (refused by the Mont-de-
Piété) with eyes half blinded by starvation;—the misery which could afford but one robe for three
marriageable daughters,—one plain dress to be worn in

---

39. "Two days—with wind."

turn by each of them, on visiting days;—the pretty misery—young, brave, sweet,—asking for a "treat" of cakes too jocosely to have its asking answered,—laughing and coquetting with its well-fed wooers, and crying for hunger after they were gone. Often and often, his heart had pleaded against his purse for such as these, and won its case in the silent courts of Self. But ever mysteriously the gift came,—sometimes as if from the hand of a former slave; sometimes as from a remorseful creditor, ashamed to write his name. Only yellow Victorine knew; but the Doctor's housekeeper never opened those sphinx-lips of hers, until years after the Doctor's name had disappeared from the City Directory. . . .

He had grown quite thin,—a little gray. The epidemic had burthened him with responsibilities too multifarious and ponderous for his slender strength to bear. The continual nervous strain of abnormally protracted duty, the perpetual interruption of sleep, had almost prostrated even his will. Now he only hoped that, during this brief absence from the city, he might find renewed strength to do his terrible task.

Mosquitoes bit savagely; and the heat became thicker;—and there was yet no wind. Sparicio and his hired boy Carmelo had been walking backward and forward for hours overhead,—urging the vessel yard by yard, with long poles, through the slime of canals and bayous. With every heavy push, the weary boy would sigh out,—"*Santo Antonio!—Santo Antonio!*" Sullen Sparicio himself at last burst into vociferations of ill-humor:—"*Santo Antonio?—Ah! santissimu e santu*

*diavulu! . . . Sacramentu pœscite vegnu un asidente!—
malidittu lu Signuri!"*[40] All through the morning they
walked and pushed, trudged and sighed and swore; and
the minutes dragged by more wearily than the shuffling
of their feet. *"Managgia Cristo co tutta a croce!"* . . .
"Santissimu e santu diavulu!!" . . .

But as they reached at last the first of the broad
bright lakes, the heat lifted, the breeze leaped up, the
loose sail flapped and filled; and, bending graciously as
a skater, the old *San Marco* began to shoot in a straight
line over the blue flood. Then, while the boy sat at the
tiller, Sparicio lighted his tiny charcoal furnace below,
and prepared a simple meal,—delicious yellow macaroni, flavored with goats' cheese; some fried fish, that
smelled appetizingly; and rich black coffee, of Oriental
fragrance and thickness. Julien ate a little, and lay
down to sleep again. This time his rest was undisturbed
by the mosquitoes; and when he woke, in the cooling
evening, he felt almost refreshed. The *San Marco* was
flying into Barataria Bay. Already the lantern in the
light-house tower had begun to glow like a little moon;
and right on the rim of the sea, a vast and vermilion sun
seemed to rest his chin. Gray pelicans came flapping
around the mast;—sea-birds sped hurtling by, their
white bosoms rose-flushed by the western glow. . . .
Again Sparicio's little furnace was at work,—more fish,
more macaroni, more black coffee; also a square-shoul-
dered bottle of gin made its appearance. Julien ate less
sparingly at this second meal; and smoked a long time

---

40. "Saint Anthony?—Ah! most saintly and devilish saint! . . . Most sacred
poet, send me an assistant!—damn the gentleman!"

on deck with Sparicio, who suddenly became very good-humored, and chatted volubly in bad Spanish, and in much worse English. Then while the boy took a few hours' sleep, the Doctor helped delightedly in manœuvering the little vessel. He had been a good yachtsman in other years; and Sparicio declared he would make a good fisherman. By midnight the *San Marco* began to run with a long, swinging gait;—she had reached deep water. Julien slept soundly; the steady rocking of the sloop seemed to soothe his nerves.

—"After all," he thought to himself, as he rose from his little bunk next morning,—"something like this is just what I needed." . . . The pleasant scent of hot coffee greeted him;—Carmelo was handing him the tin cup containing it, down through the hatchway. After drinking it he felt really hungry;—he ate more macaroni than he had ever eaten before. Then, while Sparicio slept, he aided Carmelo; and during the middle of the day he rested again. He had not had so much uninterrupted repose for many a week. He fancied he could feel himself getting strong. At supper-time it seemed to him he could not get enough to eat,—although there was plenty for everybody.

All day long there had been exactly the same wave-crease distorting the white shadow of the *San Marco*'s sail upon the blue water;—all day long they had been skimming over the liquid level of a world so jewel-blue that the low green ribbon-strips of marsh-land, the far-off fleeing lines of pine-yellow sand beach, seemed flaws or breaks in the perfected color of the universe;— all day long had the cloudless sky revealed through all its exquisite transparency that inexpressible tenderness which no painter and no poet can ever re-image,—that unutterable sweetness which no art of man may ever shadow forth, and which none may ever compre-hend,—though we feel it to be in some strange way akin to the luminous and unspeakable charm that makes us wonder at the eyes of a woman when she loves.

Evening came; and the great dominant celestial tone deepened;—the circling horizon filled with ghostly tints,—spectral greens and grays, and pearl-lights and fish-colors. . . . Carmelo, as he crouched at the tiller, was singing, in a low, clear alto, some tristful little melody. Over the sea, behind them, lay, black-stretch-ing, a long low arm of island-shore;—before them flamed the splendor of sun-death; they were sailing into a mighty glory,—into a vast and awful light of gold.

Shading his vision with his fingers, Sparicio pointed to the long lean limb of land from which they were fleeing, and said to La Brierre:—

—"Look-a, Doct-a! *Last-a Islan'!*"

Julien knew it;—he only nodded his head in reply, and looked the other way,—into the glory of God. Then, wishing to divert the fisherman's attention to another theme, he asked what was Carmelo singing. Sparicio at once shouted to the lad:—

—"Ha! . . . ho! Carmelo!—*Santu diavulu!* . . . Sing-a loud-a! Doct-a lik-a! Sing-a! sing!!" . . . "He sing-a nicee,"—added the boatman, with his peculiar dark smile. And then Carmelo sang, loud and clearly, the song he had been singing before,—one of those artless Mediterranean ballads, full of caressing vowel-sounds, and young passion, and melancholy beauty:—

> "*M' ama ancor, beltà fulgente,*
> *Come tu m' amasti allor;—*
> *Ascoltar non dei gente,*
> *Solo interroga il tuo cor.*". . .[41]

—"He sing-a nicee,—*mucha bueno!*" murmured the fisherman. And then, suddenly,—with a rich and splendid basso that seemed to thrill every fibre of the planking,—Sparicio joined in the song:—

> "*M' ama pur d'amore eterno,*
> *Nè delitto sembri a te;*
> *T' assicuro che l'inferno*
> *Una favola sol è.*". . .[42]

All the roughness of the man was gone! To Julien's startled fancy, the fishers had ceased to be;—lo! Carmelo was a princely page; Sparicio, a king! How perfectly their voices married together!—they sang with passion, with power, with truth, with that wondrous natural art which

---

41. "She still loves me, brilliant beauty,
   As you loved me then;—
   Listen not to people,
Only listen to your heart." . . . [*trans.* John Mastrigianakos]

42. "Yet she loves me with a love eternal,
   It doesn't seem a crime to you;
   I assure you that hell
Is only a fable." . . . [*trans.* John Mastrigianakos]

is the birthright of the rudest Italian soul. And the stars throbbed out in the heaven; and the glory died in the west; and the night opened its heart; and the splendor of the eternities fell all about them. Still they sang; and the *San Marco* sped on through the soft gloom, ever slightly swerved by the steady blowing of the southeast wind in her sail;—always wearing the same crimpling-frill of wave-spray about her prow,—always accompanied by the same smooth-backed swells,—always spinning out behind her the same long trail of interwoven foam. And Julien looked up. Ever the night thrilled more and more with silent twinklings;—more and more multitudinously lights pointed in the eternities;—the Evening Star quivered like a great drop of liquid white fire ready to fall;—Vega flamed as a pharos lighting the courses ethereal,—to guide the sailing of the suns, and the swarming of fleets of worlds. Then the vast sweetness of that violet night entered into his blood,—filled him with that awful joy, so near akin to sadness, which the sense of the Infinite brings,—when one feels the poetry of the Most Ancient and Most Excellent of Poets, and then is smitten at once with the contrast-thought of the sickliness and selfishness of Man,—of the blindness and brutality of cities, whereinto the divine blue light never purely comes, and the sanctification of the Silences never descends . . . furious cities, walled away from heaven. . . . Oh! if one could only sail on thus always, always through such a night—through such a star-sprinkled violet light, and hear Sparicio and Carmelo sing, even though it were the same melody always, always the same song!

. . . "Scuza, Doct-a!—look-a out!" Julien bent down, as the big boom, loosened, swung over his head. The *San Marco* was rounding into shore,—heading for her home. Sparicio lifted a huge conch-shell from the deck, put it to his lips, filled his deep lungs, and flung out into the night—thrice—a profound, mellifluent, booming horn-tone. A minute passed. Then, ghostly faint, as an echo from very far away, a triple blowing responded. . . .

And a long purple mass loomed and swelled into sight, heightened, approached—land and trees black-shadowing, and lights that swung. . . . The *San Marco* glided into a bayou,—under a high wharfing of timbers, where a bearded fisherman waited, and a woman. Sparicio flung up a rope.

The bearded man caught it by the lantern-light, and tethered the *San Marco* to her place. Then he asked, in a deep voice:

—"*¿Has traído al Doctor?*"

—"*¡Si, si!*" answered Sparicio. . . . "*¿Y el viejo?*"

—"*¡Aye! ¡pobre!*" responded Feliu,—"*hace tres días que esta muerto.*"[43]

Henry Edwards was dead!

He had died very suddenly, without a cry or a word, while resting in his rocking-chair,—the very day after Sparicio had sailed. They had made him a grave in the marsh,—among the high weeds, not far from the ruined tomb of the Spanish fisherman. But Sparicio had fairly earned his hundred dollars.

---

43. "Have you brought the Doctor?"
   "Yes, yes!. . . . and the old man?"
   "Oh, poor man, . . . he died three days ago."

V.

So there was nothing to do at Viosca's Point except to rest. Feliu and all his men were going to Barataria in the morning on business;—the Doctor could accompany them there, and take the Grand Island steamer Monday for New Orleans. With this intention Julien retired,—not sorry for being able to stretch himself at full length on the good bed prepared for him, in one of the unoccupied cabins. But he woke before day with a feeling of intense prostration, a violent headache, and such an aversion for the mere idea of food that Feliu's invitation to breakfast at five o'clock gave him an internal qualm. Perhaps a touch of malaria. In any case he felt it would be both dangerous and useless to return to town unwell; and Feliu, observing his condition, himself advised against the journey. Wednesday he would have another opportunity to leave; and in the meanwhile Carmen would take good care of him. . . . The boats departed, and Julien slept again.

The sun was high when he rose up and dressed himself, feeling no better. He would have liked to walk about the place, but felt nervously afraid of the sun. He did not remember having ever felt so broken down before. He pulled a rocking-chair to the window, tried to smoke a cigar. It commenced to make him feel still sicker, and he flung it away. It seemed to him the cabin was swaying, as the *San Marco* swayed when she first reached the deep water.

A light rustling sound approached,—a sound of quick feet treading the grass: then a shadow slanted over the threshold. In the glow of the open doorway stood a young girl,—gracile, tall,—with singularly splendid eyes,—brown eyes peeping at him from beneath a golden riot of loose hair.

—"*M'sieu-le-Docteur, maman d'mande si vous n'avez besoin d'que'que chose?*"[44] . . . She spoke the rude French of the fishing villages, where the language lives chiefly as a *baragouin*,[45] mingled often with words and forms belonging to many other tongues. She wore a loose-falling dress of some light stuff, steel-gray in color;—boys' shoes were on her feet.

He did not reply;—and her large eyes grew larger for wonder at the strange fixed gaze of the physician, whose face had visibly bleached,—blanched to corpse-pallor. Silent seconds passed; and still the eyes stared—flamed as if the life of the man had centralized and focussed within them.

His voice had risen to a cry in his throat, quivered and swelled one passionate instant, and failed—as in a dream when one strives to call, and yet can only moan. . . . *She!* Her unforgotten eyes, her brows, her lips!—the oval of her face!—the dawn-light of her hair! . . . Adèle's own poise,—her own grace!—even the very turn of her neck, even the bird-tone of her speech! . . . Had the grave sent forth a Shadow to haunt him?—could the perfidious Sea have yielded up its dead? For one

44. "Doctor, sir, mamma asks if there isn't something you need?"
45. crude spoken language

terrible fraction of a minute, memories, doubts, fears, mad fancies, went pulsing through his brain with a rush like the rhythmic throbbing of an electric stream;—then the shock passed, the Reason spoke:— "Fool!—count the long years since you first saw her thus!—count the years that have gone since you looked upon her last! And Time has never halted, silly heart!— neither has Death stood still!"

. . . "*Plait-il?*"[46]—the clear voice of the young girl asked. She thought he had made some response she could not distinctly hear.

Mastering himself an instant, as the heart faltered back to its duty, and the color remounted to his lips, he answered her in French:

—"Pardon me!—I did not hear . . . you gave me such a start!" . . . But even then another extraordinary fancy flashed through his thought;—and with the *tutoiement*[47] of a parent to a child, with an irresistible outburst of such tenderness as almost frightened her, he cried: "Oh! merciful God!—how like her! . . . Tell me, darling, your name;—tell me who you are?" (*Dis-moi qui tu es, mignonne;—dis-moi ton nom.*)

. . . Who was it had asked her the same question, in another idiom—ever so long ago? The man with the black eyes and nose like an eagle's beak,—the one who gave her the compass. Not *this* man—no!

She answered, with the timid gravity of surprise:— —"Chita Viosca."

---

46. "Please?"
47. familiarity; i.e., using the familiar form

He still watched her face, and repeated the name slowly,—reiterated it in a tone of wonderment:— "Chita Viosca?—Chita Viosca!"

—"*C'est à dire . . .*"[48] she said, looking down at her feet,—"Concha—Conchita." His strange solemnity made her smile,—the smile of shyness that knows not what else to do. But it was the smile of dead Adèle.

—"Thanks, my child," he exclaimed of a sudden,— in a quick, hoarse, changed tone. (He felt that his emotion would break loose in some wild way, if he looked upon her longer.) "I would like to see your mother this evening; but I now feel too ill to go out. I am going to try to rest a little."

—"Nothing I can bring you?" she asked,—"some fresh milk?"

—"Nothing now, dear: if I need anything later, I will tell your mother when she comes."

—"Mamma does not understand French very well."

—"*No importa, Conchita;—le hablaré en Español.*"

—"*¡Bien, entonces!*" she responded, with the same exquisite smile. "*¡Adiós, señor!*" . . . [49]

But as she turned in going, his piercing eye discerned a little brown speck below the pretty lobe of her right ear,—just in the peachy curve between neck and cheek. . . . His own little Zouzoune had a birthmark like that!—he remembered the faint pink trace left by his fingers above and below it the day he had slapped her for overturning his ink bottle. . . . "*To laimin moin?—to batté moin!*"

---

48. "That is to say . . . "
49. "It's not important, Conchita;—I'll speak to her in Spanish."
 "Well, then, . . . goodbye, sir!"

"Chita!—Chita!"

She did not hear. . . . After all, what a mistake he might have made! Were not Nature's coincidences more wonderful than fiction? Better to wait,—to question the mother first, and thus make sure.

Still—there were so many coincidences! The face, the smile, the eyes, the voice, the whole charm;—then that mark,—and the fair hair. Zouzoune had always resembled Adèle so strangely! That golden hair was a Scandinavian bequest to the Florane family;—the tall daughter of a Norwegian sea-captain had once become the wife of a Florane. Viosca?—who ever knew a Viosca with such hair? Yet again, these Spanish emigrants sometimes married blonde German girls. . . . Might be a case of atavism, too. Who was this Viosca? If that was his wife,—the little brown Carmen,—whence Chita's sunny hair? . . .

And this was part of that same desolate shore whither the Last Island dead had been drifted by that tremendous surge! On a clear day, with a good glass, one might discern from here the long blue streak of that ghastly coast. . . . Somewhere—between here and there. . . . Merciful God! . . .

. . . But again! That bivouac-night before the fight at Chancellorsville, Laroussel had begun to tell him such a singular story. . . . Chance had brought them,—the old enemies,—together; made them dear friends in the face of Death. How little he had comprehended the man!— what a brave, true, simple soul went up that day to the Lord of Battles! . . . What was it—that story about the little Creole girl saved from Last Island,—that story which was never finished? . . . Eh! what a pain!

Evidently he had worked too much, slept too little. A decided case of nervous prostration. He must lie down, and try to sleep. These pains in the head and back were becoming unbearable. Nothing but rest could avail him now.

He stretched himself under the mosquito curtain. It was very still, breathless, hot! The venomous insects were thick;—they filled the room with a continuous ebullient sound, as if invisible kettles were boiling overhead. A sign of storm. . . . Still, it was strange!—he could not perspire. . . .

Then it seemed to him that Laroussel was bending over him—Laroussel in his cavalry uniform. "*Bon jour, camarade!—nous allons avoir un bien mauvais temps, mon pauvre Julien.*" How! bad weather?—"*Comment un mauvais temps?*"[50] . . . He looked in Laroussel's face. There was something so singular in his smile. Ah! yes,—he remembered now: it was the wound! . . . "*Un vilain temps!*"[51] whispered Laroussel. Then he was gone. . . . Whither?

—"*Chéri!*" . . .

The whisper roused him with a fearful start. . . . Adèle's whisper! So she was wont to rouse him sometimes in the old sweet nights,—to crave some little attention for ailing Eulalie,—to make some little confidence she had forgotten to utter during the happy evening. . . . No, no! It was only the trees. The sky was

---

50. "Good day, comrade!—We're going to have a pretty bad storm, my poor Julien." . . . "What do you mean a bad storm?"
51. "A wicked storm!"

clouding over. The wind was rising. . . . How his heart beat! how his temples pulsed! Why, this was fever! Such pains in the back and head!

Still his skin was dry,—dry as parchment,—burning. He rose up; and a bursting weight of pain at the base of the skull made him reel like a drunken man. He staggered to the little mirror nailed upon the wall, and looked. How his eyes glowed;—and there was blood in his mouth! He felt his pulse—spasmodic, terribly rapid. Could it possibly—? . . . No: this must be some pernicious malarial fever! The Creole does not easily fall a prey to the great tropical malady,—unless after a long absence in other climates. True! he had been four years in the army! But this was 1867. . . . He hesitated a moment; then,—opening his medicine chest, he measured out and swallowed thirty grains of quinine.

Then he lay down again. His head pained more and more;—it seemed as if the cervical vertebræ were filled with fluid iron. And still his skin remained dry as if tanned. Then the anguish grew so intense as to force a groan with almost every aspiration. . . . Nausea,—and the stinging bitterness of quinine rising in his throat;—dizziness, and a brutal wrenching within his stomach. Everything began to look pink;—the light was rose-colored. It darkened more,—kindled with deepening tint. Something kept sparkling and spinning before his sight, like a firework. . . . Then a burst of blood mixed with chemical bitterness filled his mouth; the light became scarlet as claret. . . . This— this was . . . not malaria. . . .

VI.

. . . Carmen knew what it was; but the brave little woman was not afraid of it. Many a time before she had met it face to face, in Havanese summers; she knew how to wrestle with it; she had torn Feliu's life away from its yellow clutch, after one of those long struggles that strain even the strength of love. Now she feared mostly for Chita. She had ordered the girl under no circumstances to approach the cabin.

Julien felt that blankets had been heaped upon him,—that some gentle hand was bathing his scorching face with vinegar and water. Vaguely also there came to him the idea that it was night. He saw the shadow-shape of a woman moving against the red light upon the wall;—he saw there was a lamp burning.

Then the delirium seized him: he moaned, sobbed, cried like a child,—talked wildly at intervals in French, in English, in Spanish.

—"¡Mentira![52]—you could not be her mother. . . . Still, if you were—And she must not come in here,—¡jamas![53] . . . Carmen, did you know Adèle,— Adèle Florane? So like her,—so like,—God only knows how like! . . . Perhaps I think I know;—but I do not—do not know justly, fully—how like! . . . ¡Si! ¡si!—¡es el vómito!—¡yo lo conozco, Carmen! . . .[54] She must not die twice . . . I died twice. . . . I am going to die again. She only once. Till the heavens be

---

52. "A lie!"
53. "never!"
54. "Yes! yes!—it's the vomit [yellow fever]—I'm familiar with it, Carmen!"

no more she will not rise. . . . *Moi, au contraire, il faut que je me lève toujours!*[55] They need me so much;—the slate is always full; the bell will never stop. They will ring that bell for me when I am dead. . . . So will I rise again!—*resurgam!* . . . How could I save him?—could not save myself. It was a bad case,—at seventy years! . . . There! *Qui çà?"* . . .[56]

He saw Laroussel again,—reaching out a hand to him through a whirl of red smoke. He tried to grasp it, and could not. . . . *"N'importe, mon ami,"* said Laroussel,—*"tu vas la voir bientôt."*[57] Who was he to see soon?—*"qui donc, Laroussel?"*[58] But Laroussel did not answer. Through the red mist he seemed to smile;—then passed.

For some hours Carmen had trusted she could save her patient,—desperate as the case appeared to be. His was one of those rapid and violent attacks, such as often despatch their victims in a single day. In the Cuban hospitals she had seen many and many terrible examples: strong young men,—soldiers fresh from Spain,—carried panting to the fever wards at sunrise; carried to the cemeteries at sunset. Even troopers riddled with revolutionary bullets had lingered longer. . . . Still, she had believed she might save Julien's life: the burning forehead once began to bead, the burning hands grew moist.

But now the wind was moaning;—the air had become lighter, thinner, cooler. A storm was gathering

---

55. "I, to the contrary, always have to get up!"
56. "Who's that?"
57. "It's not important, my friend . . . you're going to see her soon."
58. "Who do you mean, Laroussel?"

in the east; and to the fever-stricken man the change meant death. . . . Impossible to bring the priest of the Caminada now; and there was no other within a day's sail. She could only pray; she had lost all hope in her own power to save.

Still the sick man raved; but he talked to himself at longer intervals, and with longer pauses between his words;—his voice was growing more feeble, his speech more incoherent. His thought vacillated and distorted, like flame in a wind.

Weirdly the past became confounded with the present; impressions of sight and of sound interlinked in fastastic affinity,—the face of Chita Viosca, the murmur of the rising storm. Then flickers of spectral lightning passed through his eyes, through his brain, with every throb of the burning arteries; then utter darkness came,—a darkness that surged and moaned, as the circumfluence of a shadowed sea. And through and over the moaning pealed one multitudinous human cry, one hideous interblending of shoutings and shriekings. . . . A woman's hand was locked in his own. . . . "Tighter," he muttered, "tighter still, darling! hold as long as you can!" It was the tenth night of August, eighteen hundred and fifty-six. . . .

—"*Chéri!*" . . .

Again the mysterious whisper startled him to consciousness,—the dim knowledge of a room filled with ruby-colored light,—and the sharp odor of vinegar. The house swung round slowly;—the crimson flame of the lamp lengthened and broadened by turns;—then everything turned dizzily fast,—whirled as if spinning in a vortex. . . . Nausea unutterable; and a frightful anguish as of teeth devouring him within,—tearing more and more furiously at his breast. Then one atrocious wrenching, rending, burning,—and the gush of blood burst from lips and nostrils in a smothering deluge. Again the vision of lightnings, the swaying, and the darkness of long ago. "Quick!—quick!—hold fast to the table, Adèle!—never let go!" . . .

. . . Up,—up,—up!—what! higher yet? Up to the red sky! Red—black-red . . . heated iron when its vermilion dies. So, too, the frightful flood! And noiseless. Noiseless because heavy, clammy,—thick, warm, sickening . . . blood? Well might the land quake for the weight of such a tide! . . . Why did Adèle speak Spanish? Who prayed for him? . . .

—"*¡Alma de Cristo santísima santifícame!*"

"*¡Sangre de Cristo, embriágame!*"

"*¡O buen Jesus, oye me!*" . . .[59]

Out of the darkness into—such a light! An azure haze! Ah!—the delicious frost! . . . . All the streets were filled with the sweet blue mist. . . . . Voiceless the City and white;—crooked and weed-grown its narrow ways! . . . . Old streets of tombs, these. . . . . Eh! How odd a custom!—a Night-bell at every door. Yes, of course!—a *night*-bell!—the Dead are Physicians of Souls: they may be summoned only by night,—called up from the darkness and silence. . . . Yet *she?*—might he not dare to ring for her even by day? . . . . Strange he had

---

59. "Most holy Soul of Christ, sanctify me!"

"Blood of Christ, intoxicate me!"

"Oh good Jesus, hear me!"

deemed it day!—why, it was black, starless. . . . And it was growing queerly cold. . . . . How should he ever find her now? It was so black . . . so cold! . . .

—"*Chéri!*"

All the dwelling quivered with the mighty whisper.

Outside, the great oaks were trembling to their roots;—all the shore shook and blanched before the calling of the sea.

And Carmen, kneeling at the feet of the dead, cried out, alone in the night:—

—"*¡O Jesus misericordioso!—¡tened compasión de él!*"[60]

---

60. "Oh merciful Jesus!—you had compassion for him!"